THE DONOR

SANDI LYNN

SANDI LYNN ROMANCE, LLC

THE DONOR

New York Times, USA Today & Wall Street Journal
Bestselling Author
Sandi Lynn

The Donor

Copyright © 2020 Sandi Lynn Romance, LLC

All rights reserved. No part of this publication may be reproduced, distributed, or transmitted in any form or by any means, including photocopying, recording, or other electronic or mechanical methods without the prior written permission of the publisher.
This is a work of fiction. Names, characters, places and incidents are the products of the authors imagination or are used fictitiously. Any resemblance to actual events, locales, or persons, living or dead, is entirely coincidental.

※ Created with Vellum

MISSION STATEMENT

Sandi Lynn Romance

Providing readers with romance novels that will whisk them away to another world and from the daily grind of life – one book at a time.

PROLOGUE

*G*rayson

"It's not too late to back out. The limo is outside. Just say the word and we'll go. You don't have to do this."

"Grayson, come on. I love Yasmin. You know I do," Julius spoke as he straightened his bowtie in the mirror.

"No, bro. You don't. You just think you do. Hell, you don't know what love is and now you're throwing your entire life away based on a fucking one-night stand you had six months ago."

"You," he pointed at me, "have no clue what it's like to love someone. I didn't either until I met her. Trust me, Grayson, this is real, and I'm not going anywhere."

"Bullshit! I will not stand here and watch my best friend throw his life away over some damn chick. I'll bet that you two don't make it to your second anniversary."

"Fine. It's a bet," he spoke. "And here's what we're betting."

What he proposed was preposterous and shocked me.

"What's wrong, Grayson? Too chicken? Don't have the balls to accept? If you're so sure I won't make it then you won't have any problem accepting the bet."

I stared at him for I knew my best friend better than anybody in

1

the world. We'd been glued to each other's side since we were eight years old and we'd been through a lot of shit together over the years. I knew him well enough that I wouldn't be the one losing the bet.

"Fine. It's a bet," I spoke.

"Good. If I lose, you have my word that I will complete our bet," he said. "And I want your word that you will complete yours if you lose." His brow arched.

"You have my word." I held out my hand for a bro shake. "Two years."

The one thing I took pride in was that if I gave someone my word, I meant it. My word was something I never backed down from.

CHAPTER 1

TWO YEARS LATER

Grayson

"Mhm." I heard as her arm wrapped tightly around my waist.

Removing her arm, I sat up with my back to her and my feet planted firmly on the floor as I rubbed my aching head.

"Last night was amazing. How about an encore?" the woman whose name I couldn't remember for the life of me spoke.

"I can't. I have to get to the office, and you need to go."

I headed into the bathroom and started the shower. Shortly after I stepped in, the door opened. Immediately, I grabbed it shut.

"Sorry, love. I shower alone."

"Are you serious, Grayson?"

"I'm very serious. Go make us some coffee."

When I finished, I wrapped a towel around my waist, grabbed my wallet out of my pants pocket and checked to make sure all my credit cards and cash were still intact before I kicked her out. Walking into the kitchen, I grabbed the cup of coffee she had waiting for me on the island.

"Thanks. Why aren't you dressed yet?" I asked as she stood there in my t-shirt.

"I don't know." She smiled as she ran her finger down my chest. "I thought maybe after your shower you'd change your mind."

"I haven't changed my mind and I don't have time for this," I spoke as I went into the bedroom, gathered her clothes and threw them at her. "Listen, I don't even remember your name. We had a good time last night, and that was it. One time is all it'll be."

"Wow. You're a dick," she spoke with irritation as she slipped on her dress.

"What did you really expect? We met in a club and you were an easy fuck. If you're looking for something more, stop having sex with random guys you've only known for five minutes. You're the one giving yourself a cheap and easy reputation. If that's how you put yourself out there, that's how guys will treat you. Now if you'll excuse me, I have to get ready for work."

"Fuck you, Grayson!" she shouted as she grabbed her shoes and stormed into the elevator.

I rolled my eyes and went into the bedroom to get dressed. It was the same conversation every single time. But I preferred women like her because it was easy to get rid of them. Any woman on my level would want more.

I was in the public eye more than I wanted to be. But when you're New York's number one bachelor, it was hard not to. Being the right hand of my grandfather who built Rhodes Enterprises was stressful. A stress I managed by partying every night and meeting different women that I could use to my advantage and then send home the next morning.

※

"Morning, Christine. Coffee now," I said to my secretary as I walked past her desk and into my office.

"Right away, Mr. Rhodes."

Setting my briefcase down, I took a seat behind my desk and logged onto my computer, pulling up the acquisition notes for a project I was working on.

"Here you go," Christine spoke as she set the cup on my desk.

"Thanks. Clear my schedule from twelve to one thirty. I'm having lunch with Julius today."

"Will do, Mr. Rhodes."

As I was absorbed into my work, my phone dinged with a text message from Damon, my driver.

"I'm here."

"I'll be down in a second."

Shutting down my computer, I grabbed my suit coat and headed out of the building where Damon was waiting for me with the door open.

"Where are you meeting Julius for lunch?" he asked.

"Pastis in the Meatpacking District," I replied as I climbed inside.

"Your grandfather phoned me this morning." His eyes peered at me through the rearview mirror.

"What did he want?"

"He wanted to know your whereabouts last night."

"What did you tell him?"

"I told him I took you home from the office and if you went anywhere after that, I didn't know."

"Thanks, Damon." I smiled.

I climbed out of the Escalade and headed inside Pastis, where a cute brunette walked me over to where Julius sat. He stood up, and we lightly hugged.

"I already ordered you a bourbon, and I made it a double." He smirked.

"Thanks. A double?"

"Do you know what today is?" he asked.

"Monday?" I arched my brow.

"It is Monday, but it's also something else."

Our waitress walked over and set our drinks down in front of us. After placing our order, I picked up my bourbon and took a sip.

"Are you going to tell me what today is, or do I have to keep guessing?"

"It's mine and Yasmin's second wedding anniversary." A grin crossed his face.

Oh shit.

"Is that so, I sipped on my bourbon."

"It is and we're still going strong and as in love as ever. So, Grayson, you know what that means." The look on his face turned serious.

"It means I lost the bet." I finished my drink and signaled the waitress to bring me another.

"Indeed, it does. And it's time for me to collect."

A sick feeling washed over me as I stared at him.

"What's wrong? Suddenly, you're as pale as a ghost." He smirked.

"Nothing."

As the waitress walked over with my drink, she also brought us our food.

"If there's anything else you gentlemen need, just ask." She winked at me.

"Listen, bro. You gave me your word. It's time to pay up."

"I'm really surprised at you, Julius. I honestly didn't think you'd make it. Why don't we extend the bet to three years?"

"Hell no." He laughed. "You said we wouldn't make it to our second anniversary, and we did. You lost, I won, and now you'll honor our bet. So, I'll get everything started on my end after lunch. I'll expect you in my office tomorrow morning." He smiled.

"One month, Julius. We agreed that if I lost, it would only be for one month."

"You're right and it will be. You have my word. Plus, I'll bury you in the back so the chances of someone finding your profile will literally be zero."

"I'm trusting you, Julius. I'll be by your office tomorrow morning."

CHAPTER 2

*H*arper

It was on my thirtieth birthday that I made my final decision to do something I wanted my whole life. There wasn't any question or doubt in my mind. I'd had enough of men and the constant heartbreak that followed. The final straw was when my fiancé, Kevin, called it quits three months before we were to be married. He sat me down one night and told me he just wasn't one hundred percent sure I was the one he wanted to spend the rest of his life with. He told me he still loved me, but maybe not enough for the rest of our lives. As you could imagine, it broke me beyond belief. We lost all the deposits we had put down on everything and my wedding dress was nonrefundable. So not only was I out a shitload of money, I was alone and heartbroken beyond repair.

"Are you one hundred percent sure you want to do this?" my best friend Charlotte asked.

"Yeah, Harper? This isn't something you can back out of if you change your mind. Once it's done, it's done," my other best friend, Laurel spoke.

"I know that. Come on. We've known each other since college. You know me and you know what I've always dreamed of."

"Yes. We know," Charlotte spoke. "But you'll meet the right guy who will love and cherish you and want the same thing."

"You still have time, Harper. You're only thirty years old," Laurel said.

"And we can see how well things have worked out for me. The clock is ticking away, and this is what I want."

"Raising a child alone and on your own will be hard," Laurel said.

"Technically, she won't be alone," Charlotte spoke. "She has us."

"I know, but you know what I mean."

"Why the hell do I need a man to raise a child? Men are basically children themselves and need to be taken care of. This is what I want and I'm doing it. With or without your support."

Both Charlotte and Laurel got up from their seats, walked over to me, and gave me a hug.

"We'll always support your decisions no matter what," Charlotte said.

"And we'll always be here for you." Laurel hugged me tight.

CHAPTER 3

ONE MONTH LATER

Grayson

I was sitting at my desk going over some contracts when my phone rang.

"Hey, Julius."

"Grayson, can you come to my office? I have everything back."

I sighed. "When?"

"I can see you in an hour."

"Fine. I'll be there but you better have some bourbon on hand."

"Will do, bro." He laughed. "See you soon."

I ended the call and leaned back in my chair as I threw my pen across my desk. This was humiliating and I wouldn't be in this position if Julius would have gotten divorced before the two years were up. Fuck my life.

"I'm heading to meet Julius. I should be back in a couple of hours," I spoke to Christine as I passed by her desk.

"Don't forget you have a meeting at two o'clock."

"I haven't forgotten." I sighed.

"Good morning, Mr. Rhodes." Brianna, his secretary smiled as she bit down on her bottom lip.

"Good morning, beautiful." I winked. "He's expecting me."

"He told me to tell you to have a seat and he'll be back in a few minutes. Can I get you some coffee?" She flirted.

"I'd love some."

She got up from her seat and I watched her strut her sexy body down the hallway to the break room. Damn. What I wouldn't give to fuck her. But I was under strict instructions from Julius that she was off limits. I figured he wanted her for himself, but it turned out he was only protecting her from me.

As I took a seat across from his desk, I picked up the picture of him and Yasmin. Rolling my eyes, I set it down as Brianna stepped in and handed me my coffee.

"Here you go, Mr. Rhodes." She smiled. "If there's anything else I can give you, all you have to do is ask. I would never say no."

"Brianna, that's enough. Shut the door on your way out," Julius spoke as he walked in.

"How the fuck have you never stuck your dick in her yet?" I asked.

"Because I'm in love and I'm married. But you wouldn't know anything about that." He cocked his head. "And again I will warn you. Whatever filthy ideas you have running through that head of yours where Brianna is concerned, just stop. You are not to even look at her."

"You're such a fucking cock blocker. Now why am I here?"

"I have all of your test results." He grinned as he held up a file folder.

"And?"

"First things first. Never fuck without a condom. Your sperm are some of the best I've seen in a long time. Strong and fast."

"Of course they are." A smirk crossed my lips.

"Second, your genetic screening came back perfect. I would tend to disagree, but the test results don't lie. And you're clean. No trace of any sexually transmitted diseases. Which surprised me with the women you sleep with."

"You're a douchebag, Julius." I narrowed my eye at him.

He gave me a smile and continued.

"I need you to sign this waiver of parental rights form. Even though we'll never need it, I need you to sign it. It's just a formality, and it will be trashed with everything else in a month."

"I can't fucking believe I agreed to this." I picked up a pen and signed the form.

"You need to be careful with your words, my friend. A bet is a bet. Here is your profile. I took the liberty of writing it for you." He handed me the paper.

"Where the fuck did you get this picture of me when I was three?" I asked.

"Celia gave it to me."

"My grandfather's housekeeper?" I cocked my head.

"Yeah. I stopped by and told her I was putting a collage together for a party I was throwing you." He laughed.

"Jesus Christ." I shook my head.

"Don't worry. Like I said, no one will even see it."

"I like the way you made me sound here," I said as I read over my profile. "You make me sound like an awesome guy." A smirk crossed my lips.

"Yeah. I know." He rolled his eyes. "Anyway, like I said before no one will even see it. I'll make sure it's buried. Just making you do this is enough for me." He laughed. "We'll be laughing about this in the years to come, my friend."

"Somehow I doubt it." I narrowed my eye at him.

"Oh, I'm taking Yasmin to Aruba for our second anniversary, so I'll be gone about ten days."

"Your anniversary was last month."

"I know, but Yasmin couldn't get the time off work then."

"What happened to you?" I shook my head at him.

"Cupid happened. Maybe it'll happen to you one day."

"When cupid comes my way, I'll be shooting that little bastard down fast," I said as I got up from my seat.

"Don't knock it until you've tried it, Grayson. It's a pretty powerful feeling."

"I have all the power I need, bro. I'll talk to you later."

CHAPTER 4

Harper

I took in a deep breath as I stepped through the doors of the New York Cryobank.

"Hello, how may I help you?" an older woman with a pleasant smile asked.

"I have an appointment with Larson Whitfield."

"Your name, please."

"Harper Holland."

"Ah yes. Here you are. Follow me and I'll take you to him."

I followed her down the hallway and we entered the last office on the right.

"Mr. Whitfield, Harper Holland is here."

"Please, come in and have a seat. It's nice to meet you, Miss Holland." He graciously extended his hand.

"Thank you. It's nice to meet you, Mr. Whitfield." I placed my hand in his.

After taking a seat across from his desk, he sat down in his chair and opened up a folder.

"So," he folded his hands. "You want to have a baby."

"Yes." I smiled.

"Excellent. We can definitely help you." He grinned. "Here's a folder with all of our information, costs, and a sheet for you to fill out with exactly what you're looking for. Eye color, hair color, height, weight, race and a few other things. Once you fill that out and turn it in, we'll email you a link to all the donors who match what you're looking for with a comprehensive background and you can view them online. Once you find your perfect donor, all you have to do is add the donor to your cart, check out and we can either mail the sperm to you, you can come in and pick it up yourself or you can schedule an appointment with one of our fertility experts and have the insemination done here. It costs a little extra, but a lot of our customers take advantage of that if they don't want their doctors to know they're using a donor."

"Wow. So it's kind of like online shopping." I smirked.

"Yes." He chuckled. "We want to make the experience the best and easiest way possible for you."

"I've already made a list of what I would like," I spoke as I pulled the piece of paper from my purse and handed it to him.

"Excellent. I will get this information keyed in under your file and you should be receiving an email from us with the link in about forty-eight hours."

"That's it?" I asked with surprise.

"That's it, Miss Holland. It was a pleasure meeting you." He stood up from his chair and extended his hand.

"Thank you, Mr. Whitfield. I can't wait to start my search."

"This is so weird to me," Charlotte spoke as she poured more wine in her glass. "Who would have thought you could order your kid online."

"Pour me another glass and then get your ass over here. I'm clicking the link," I said.

She handed me my wine and took a seat on the couch next to me while Laurel was on the other side. Nervously, I clicked the link in my email from the cryobank, and a webpage opened with a list of pictures and donor numbers.

"Why are all these pictures of kids?" Laurel asked. "I thought we'd get to see the donor."

"It must be the donor when they were a child. Which makes sense because my child would look like a part of them," I said.

I clicked on a few donors and read their profiles.

"Why do they all have brown hair and blue eyes?" Laurel asked.

"That's what I requested. I have brown hair and blue eyes. Plus, you know that's my type, anyway."

After a couple hours of drinking wine and scouring through donors, Charlotte and Laurel left, and I changed into my pajamas and climbed in bed to do some work. I would finish looking through the donors tomorrow. As I was finalizing a design and getting ready to send it off to the company who hired me, an email came through from the cryobank. The email contained a link to a new donor that was just listed with the characteristics I was looking for. Clicking on the link, I began reading about Donor 137665.

Donor 137665 is a highly educated top of his class graduate from Yale. With his high I.Q. and competitive nature, he is extremely successful in the corporate business world. He has an outgoing personality and loves to socialize and meet new people. As an avid classical music lover, he relaxes by sitting down and playing music by Beethoven and Bach on his grand piano.

Height – 6'2
Weight – 190lbs.
Eye Color – Blue
Hair Color – Brown
Hair texture – Straight
Ethnic Origin – Caucasian
Ancestry – English, Irish, Scottish
Religion – None
Education Level – Masters
Areas of Study – Business, Finance, Investment Management
Blood Type – O+

Pregnancies – No
Expanded Genetic Testing – Yes
Instruments – Piano
Favorite Food – Mexican, Italian
Outdoor fun – Skiing and walks on the beach.

I repeatedly read his profile and stared at his picture. He was a super handsome little boy. I only wish I could see what he looked like now. I couldn't stop yawning so I closed my laptop and went to sleep.

CHAPTER 5

Harper

When I awoke the next morning, I grabbed my laptop and took it to the kitchen while I made a cup of coffee. Upon opening it, the tab with the donor information I was viewing last night stared me straight in the face. He was the one. I felt it last night, and I felt it this morning. Every time I looked over his profile, I knew he would be the perfect man to father my child.

I took a sip of my coffee as I added him, entered my credit card information and stared at the "Complete Purchase" button. I hovered over it, hesitating for a moment. This was it. Once I clicked that button, there was no going back. But I knew in my heart this was exactly what I wanted. What I've always wanted. I took in a long deep breath as I clicked the purchase button. A confirmation screen appeared in front of me, and it was done. I had just ordered my baby.

Picking up my phone, I gave Mr. Whitfield a call for I wanted to have it done at the cryobank.

"Larson Whitfield," he answered.

"Good morning, Mr. Whitfield. This is Harper Holland. I met with you a few days ago."

"Yes, Miss Holland. How are you?"

"I'm good. I just wanted to let you know that I found the donor I want, and I placed an order for the sperm. I would like to come in and have the procedure done at your center."

"Excellent. You're not on the pill or any other form of birth control, are you?"

"No. I've been off the pill for about seven months."

"Good. The next step will be to come in when you're ovulating. You must go buy an ovulation kit and then come in during your fertile window. We know this is a time sensitive matter, so we'll get you in immediately. Just call our number and tell the receptionist that you're ovulating, and she'll take care of the rest."

"Thank you, Mr. Whitfield."

"You're welcome, Miss Holland. Good luck to you."

I ended the call and finished my coffee before hopping in the shower and getting dressed for the day. I had a meeting with a software company to redesign their website, so I'd stop at the drugstore on the way back and pick up an ovulation kit. I couldn't believe this was happening and with any luck, I'd soon be pregnant and have the family I'd always wanted.

After my meeting with the software company, I stopped at the drugstore, picked up an ovulation kit, and then sent Laurel and Charlotte a group text message.

"I picked a donor. Can you meet for dinner tonight?"

"OMG! Where and what time?" Laurel replied.

"Holy Shit! I'm in. Let me know the details." Charlotte wrote.

"Loring Place. Six o'clock."

&

I was about fifteen minutes late to meet the girls due to an unexpected business call I had.

"Sorry I'm late," I spoke as I took a seat. "The software company I met with this morning hired me and we had to go over a few things via phone."

"So, tell us who the baby daddy is." Charlotte grinned.

"How did you pick one so fast?" Laurel asked.

I pulled out my phone, signed into my cryobank account and pulled up Donor 137665.

"This is him." I smiled as I handed them my phone.

"Wow. He has a high I.Q." Laurel said.

"I love a man who can play the piano." Charlotte swooned. "He sounds perfect and dreamy. And you also play the piano. Your child could be a musical genius."

"I'd take his sperm, but I'd want it the old fashion way." Laurel grinned.

"So now what happens?" Charlotte asked.

"Well, I've decided to have the insemination done at the cryobank. This facility has a doctor on staff who does the procedure. I have to call them when I'm ovulating."

"And when will that be?" Laurel asked.

"According to my period app, I'll be ovulating in three days. I also bought an ovulating test kit. When I'm in my fertile window, I call the center and they'll get me right in."

"You better let us know so we both can be there with you," Charlotte spoke.

"Yeah. We're not letting you go through this alone," Laurel said.

I reached across the table and grabbed hold of their hands.

"Thank you. I love you both so much."

"We love you." Charlotte started to tear up. "I can't believe you're actually doing this."

"I know. It doesn't seem real yet. I was also thinking I need to move."

"Why?" Laurel asked.

"My apartment is only a one bedroom. I'll need a two bedroom for the baby."

"Can you afford a two bedroom?"

"I don't have a choice. I'll just have to make sure I budget and try to pick up a few more accounts."

"Don't forget about all the medical bills you'll have coming up," Charlotte said.

"I know and my insurance only covers half. But I'll manage. I always have." I softly smiled.

CHAPTER 6

SIX WEEKS LATER

Grayson

Rolling over, I looked at the woman sleeping next to me and sighed. I picked my pants up off the hotel room floor and slipped them on. As I was buttoning my shirt, she stirred. Shit. I wanted to make my escape before she woke up.

"Where are you going?" I heard her hungover voice speak.

"Home. I need to shower and change clothes."

"What's the rush? The least you could do is buy me breakfast."

"Order room service. But make it for one. I'm out of here. I already paid for the room, so you don't need to worry."

"Seriously? You're just going to leave like that? I thought we had a good time last night."

"We did and now it's over. I have things to do."

"Am I ever going to see you again, Grayson?"

"No, Molly. Last night was a one-time thing."

"It's Holly, you asshole!"

"Right. Sorry." I sat on the edge of the bed and put my shoes on. "Thanks for last night. Have a good day," I spoke as I grabbed my phone from the nightstand and left the room.

Climbing into the Escalade parked at the curb, I told Damon to take me home. Just as he pulled up, my phone rang, and it was Julius.

"What's up?"

"Grayson, are you home or at the office?"

"I just got home. Why?"

"I'm heading over there now. We need to talk."

"Is everything okay?" I asked.

"I'll explain when I get there."

Placing my phone in my pocket, I climbed out and stepped into the building.

"Good morning, Mr. Rhodes." The doorman smiled.

"Good morning, Charlie."

Stepping into the elevator, I took it up to the penthouse. I kept thinking about Julius and how panicked his voice sounded. What the hell happened? Maybe he was coming to tell me that him and Yasmin were breaking up. Or maybe he was coming to tell me he cheated on her. Either way, I'd find out in a few minutes when he got here.

I went upstairs to my bedroom and changed into a pair of sweatpants and t-shirt. I'd shower after he left. As I was in the kitchen making a cup of coffee, I heard the elevator door open.

"Hey. Coffee?" I asked as he stepped into the kitchen.

"No." He put up his hand.

"What's going on?"

He placed his hands in pants pockets and began pacing around the room.

"Julius, what the hell is going on?"

"There's something I have to tell you and you're not going to like it."

"Okay. Just calm down and tell me."

"You better sit first."

He walked over to the bar, poured a glass of bourbon, took the coffee cup from my hand, and handed me the glass.

"What the hell?" I looked up at him.

"Trust me. You'll need that." He began pacing again.

"For fuck sakes, Julius. Fucking tell me what's going on!" I shouted.

"Someone purchased your sperm and now she's pregnant."

"WHAT!" I shouted as I stood up. "How did that happen? YOU promised me it wouldn't!"

"I don't know, Grayson. I'm still trying to find that out. Apparently, you matched exactly what this woman was looking for and they sent your profile to her. I'm still investigating and when I find out exactly who did it, they're fired."

"How do you know? Are you one hundred percent sure?" I threw the warm liquid down my throat.

"I was going over the list of donors and pregnancies for the month and I saw your donor number listed."

"FUCK! You're the goddamn director of that facility! How could you let this happen? Didn't you take it down after a month like you promised me you would?"

"YES! I took it down immediately. It happened when I was in Aruba."

"Now what?" I threw back the rest of my drink and slammed the glass down on the bar. "What the fuck am I supposed to do now?"

"Nothing. There's nothing you can do. If I were you, I'd forget about it. Pretend it never happened."

"Right. Pretend it never happened. BUT IT DID! And now there's some woman out there in the world carrying my kid!"

"Actually, she's right here in New York."

Placing my hand on my forehead, I slowly shook my head.

"Listen, Grayson. There are a million donors out there. You're not responsible for the kid in any way and since you were listed as anonymous with no contact, she will never know you're the father. Ever. Just forget about it, bro. You can do that. It's no big deal. In fact, look at it this way, you made a woman who so badly wanted a child happy. You gave her the greatest gift of life and the best part is you aren't being held responsible for the kid."

I stood there and narrowed my eye at him as I slowly shook my head.

"Grayson, listen to what I said. Just forget it even happened. It's not like you fucked her and it was an accident. You're not responsible for this. You're not, nor will you ever be tied to this woman and the child. You know, I didn't even have to tell you. I could have kept this from you and you never would have known. But I told you because you're my best friend and I couldn't keep it from you. I have to go. I told Yasmin I wouldn't be long. We're going to her mother's for brunch. I'm sorry, bro." He turned around and stepped into the elevator.

Walking over to the bar, I poured myself another drink. This was fucking unbelievable. I stood in the shower as I let the stream of hot water pour over me. I kept replaying our conversation repeatedly in my head. Julius was right. I just had to put it out of my mind, forget about it and pretend our conversation never took place. I never should have agreed to the bet in the first place. Of all the mistakes I've made in my life, this one was by far the worst of them all.

CHAPTER 7

Grayson

I was sitting behind my desk when my grandfather walked in.

"Grandfather," I spoke in shock.

"Hello, Grayson."

Getting up from my chair, I walked over and gave him a hug.

"When did you get back from Europe?"

"Last night. I'd like you to come over for dinner tonight. I have something I want to talk to you about."

"Okay. Sure. Is everything okay?"

"Yeah. We just haven't had a good talk in a while. I'll see you at seven."

"See you then."

He walked out and Christine walked in.

"Did you know he was back?" she asked.

"No. I didn't." My brows furrowed.

"Glenn Sharpe called." She handed me the message. "He needs you to call him right away."

"Great." I rolled my eyes.

The moment I walked into my grandfather's home, Celia greeted me with a hug.

"It's good to see you, Grayson."

"It's good to see you too, Celia." I smiled.

"Your grandfather is in the living room. Dinner will be ready in a few minutes."

"Thank you."

I walked into the living room and found my grandfather sitting in his favorite chair with a drink in his hand.

"Hello, Grayson."

"Grandfather." I nodded.

"Go pour yourself a drink and have a seat."

Walking over to the bar, I poured myself a bourbon and took it over to the couch.

"What did you want to talk to me about?" I asked.

"Are you seeing anyone special? Perhaps you've met someone while I was away?"

"No." I furrowed my brows at him. "Why?"

"Excuse me, Mr. Rhodes. Dinner is ready," Celia spoke as she entered the living room.

We both got up and took our seats in the dining room.

"Why are you asking, Grandfather?"

"I've been keeping a close eye on things while I was away. An eye on the business and an eye on you. It seems you haven't slowed down at all as far as the partying and women are concerned."

"And?" I narrowed my eye at him. "What I do on my personal time has no effect on my job or performance. You can see that."

"That is true, Grayson. The deals you've closed and the decisions you've made regarding the company have been impeccable. You're going to be thirty-two years old. Don't you think it's time you thought about settling down? Find a special woman you can share your life with?"

"No, Grandfather, I don't think that. You know how I am."

"And I've overlooked it the past few years because I thought it was just a phase. But like I said, you're going to be thirty-two years old. I married your grandmother when I was twenty-one and started a family when I was twenty-two."

"That was fifty-years ago. Times have changed. People have changed. Views about relationships and marriage aren't the same anymore. What exactly are you trying to say?"

"Family is important, and I think the key to a solid exceptional businessman is the family he has supporting him. You know I'm retiring in a year."

"Yes. I know."

"You're my grandson and I love you very much. But your partying and excess use of women is out of control. I'm giving you one solid year to find someone to love and build a life with."

"What?!" I exclaimed. "And if I don't?"

"Then I have no choice but to sign the company over to Alfie."

"Alfie? You can't be serious! That pompous ass couldn't run a company on his own if it was shoved up his ass!"

"He's doing just fine, and he has a great wife who supports him."

"Yeah. Under me and with my guidance. His wife has nothing to do with his job performance."

"Sure it does. A happy man makes you better. If I didn't have your grandmother by my side when I started the business and over the years, I probably wouldn't have made it."

"This is utterly ridiculous! I can't believe you, Grandfather."

"And I can't believe you, Grayson. It's time to grow the fuck up and have some stability in your life."

"I have stability, and I'll be damned if I'm going to let you sign the company over to Alfie. I've worked my ass off to get where I am today. That is MY company." I pointed at him. "You've been grooming me to take over since I was a teenager."

"And it will be yours as long as you adhere to my request. You're missing out on so much more in life."

"I'm missing nothing and I'm doing just fine. I enjoy my life and the way I live it. You cannot sit there and tell me what to do! This is MY life!" I shouted.

"You're right. Only you have the power to create your destiny. But it is my company and I can do what I want with it. You have one year, Grayson. Enough with these trashy women you're spending your nights with. I no longer want to see your name at the top of New York's most eligible bachelor's list. And if you think you can pull a fast one on me and drum someone up just for show, you're seriously mistaken." He pointed at me. "My intention from the day you were born was to have you take over the family business and I want that legacy continued for generations to come. But I will not hand my company over to someone who never intends on making that happen." He got up from the table. "It was a pleasure having dinner with you again. It's been way too long. The fate of your future is in your hands, Grayson." He walked out of the dining room.

I slammed my fist down on the table. Rage consumed me and I needed to get the fuck out of here. Dialing Damon, I told him to come get me.

"Are you okay, Mr. Rhodes?" Celia asked. "I overheard part of your conversation."

"No, Celia. I'm not okay! He's being an asshole! What the hell is wrong with him?!"

"I'm sure he's just trying to look out for your best interest."

"Well, he needs to stay the fuck out of my life." I got up and kissed her cheek. "Have a good night," I spoke as I walked out the door.

CHAPTER 8

Harper
I stared at my naked body in the full-length mirror and placed my hands on my belly. I couldn't believe I was pregnant and had a living being inside of me. To be honest, I didn't think it would happen on the first try. But it did and I was the happiest I'd ever been in my life. I was six weeks along and now it was time to put my plans in motion. Not only did I have to hunt for a new apartment, I needed to secure some more accounts for my graphic design business.

I had three apartment tours lined up for today. After stopping at Starbuck's and grabbing a decaf coffee, I headed to my first appointment. I wasn't impressed at all. The pictures online were much more appealing. My second apartment tour was an apartment I fell in love with, but it was way out of my budget range, and the third, same as the first. I wouldn't allow myself to get discouraged just yet. I'd find the perfect apartment for me and my child. All I needed was a little patience and more accounts.

"Have you considered just going to work for a company?" Charlotte asked. "I know how much you hate that kind of structure and office setting, but I'm not sure you have a choice now."

"I have, but nobody will hire me being pregnant. Shit. The two bedroom apartments in this city are so costly and I refuse to raise my kid in a sketchy neighborhood. I'll just have to drum up more business."

When I got home, I was exhausted, so I laid down and took a three-hour nap. When I awoke and checked my phone, I had a voicemail from the director of a marketing firm I'd been steadily doing work for.

"Harper, It's Connie. Listen, I have some bad news. Things right now aren't good for us, so we have to scale back and cut costs. Unfortunately, we won't be needing your services anymore. I'm sorry. You're so talented and your work is exceptional. I'm sure you won't have a problem finding another firm to do work for. I'm putting your final check in the mail today. I'm so sorry about this."

A sickness formed in the pit of my belly as I listened to her message. That marketing firm was my bread and butter. They were my top account. Without them, I had just lost half of my income. Tears started to stream down my face as fear crept inside me. This wasn't only about me anymore. I had a baby to think about. This couldn't have happened at the worst time. But at least they owed me a chunk of money. Money that would get me through at least another month.

Grayson

I took my bourbon over to my piano and set it down. Taking a seat on the bench, I placed my fingers on the keys and began playing. What the fuck was I going to do? I never hated my grandfather more than I did at this moment. I wasn't a relationship type of guy. I gave all that up in college. Women were too much of a problem for me. They didn't understand I had a life outside of them. That I was working hard for my future. All the fighting and the yelling because I didn't spend enough time with them or pay them enough attention was exhausting. It was then I decided to stay single. I was better off without all that complication in my life and my grandfather couldn't understand that. He couldn't understand that I was better off being single. I liked women for one thing and one thing only: the pleasure they provided me with sex. It was all I needed. I was a happy man living the bachelor life and doing whatever the fuck I wanted to do without someone trying to control me. But now, he was the one controlling me. He was in control of my future and I didn't like it one bit. But I'd never let Alfie take control of the company I worked so hard to make mine.

CHAPTER 9

Grayson

It had been a week since I met with my grandfather, and now the clock was ticking away. I hadn't told Julius yet, and I needed to talk to someone. Then suddenly, a lightbulb went off in my head. Julius was the key to this whole thing. Picking up my phone, I dialed him.

"Hey, Grayson."

"Can you come by the penthouse tonight? We haven't had a bro night in a while. I'll order us a couple pizzas and we can kick back and drink a few beers. That's if Yasmin will let you out of the house."

"Hilarious, Grayson. It just so happens I was going to call you and ask you the same thing. Yasmin is going out with her friends tonight. What time do you want me over?"

"How about seven o'clock?"

"Sounds good. I'll bring the beer."

"Great. I'll see you tonight."

I ended the call and set my phone down. I prayed to God that he would tell me what I wanted to hear.

The elevator door opened and when I walked into the foyer, Julius stepped out.

"Hey, bro." We lightly hugged.

"How are you, Grayson? We really haven't spoken much the past couple of weeks. I was afraid you were ending our friendship."

"Nah, Julius. You're like my brother. No matter what, I could never stop being your friend." I smiled. "The pizza is on the island."

"And I brought the beer." He held up a six-pack.

Walking to the kitchen, I reached up into the cabinet and took down two plates. Grabbing two slices of pizza from the box and a bottle of beer, I took it over to the table.

"How are you, man?" Julius asked as he took the seat across from me.

"I've been wanting to tell you what's going on, but first I had to calm the fuck down and process it."

"Process what? What happened?"

"I had dinner with my grandfather last week."

"I didn't know he was back in town."

"I didn't either until he showed up at the office. He invited me to dinner. Boy, I had no idea what I was in for that night."

He steadily narrowed his eye at me as he brought the bottle up to his lips.

"What the fuck happened?"

"My grandfather thinks it's time I grow the fuck up and have some stability in my life. He claims that my partying and women reputation is out of hand. He's giving me one year to find a woman to fall in love with, and if I don't, he's signing the company over to Alfie."

"What?" He choked before spitting out the beer in his mouth. "You can't be serious, Grayson."

"Oh, I'm dead serious."

"So if you don't get in a relationship or fall in love before the one-year mark, the company isn't yours?"

"That's right."

"What the fuck is his problem? What does it matter to him? You're running that company to perfection. You've more than proved yourself to him."

"I know." I shook my head. "He wants the company to be a family legacy. And without me having a family, that won't happen."

"So he'd just give it to Alfie? I don't get it." Julius furrowed his brows.

"He has a wife and two kids."

"But he's not family."

"Trust me. I know that, Julius. I don't understand why my grandfather is being like this."

"So what are you going to do?"

I took a sip of my beer as I stared at him.

"The woman who used my sperm. Is she single or married?"

"Oh fuck no, Grayson. No way." He shook his head. "I can't tell you that." He placed his hands on his head. "Oh my God, I know what you're thinking, and the answer is no!"

"You owe me!" I spoke through gritted teeth. "You made a promise to me that my sperm would never be found by someone to use, and you failed!" I pointed at him. "You got me in this mess, and now you will get me out of the current one I'm in with my grandfather."

"Have you forgotten that you signed off all parental rights to that kid? What the hell are you going to do? Go to the woman and tell her you need your kid after all?"

I took in a deep breath to calm down.

"I have a plan, but I need to know if she's single or married. Please, Julius. I need your help. I could lose everything."

"Shit, Grayson." A worried look crossed his face. "You can't disrupt this woman's life to save your own. It's not right. Plus, I could get fired if anyone found out. Not to mention that this woman could sue the shit out of us."

"Your family owns the sperm bank. You're the director, the overseer. I'll make sure she doesn't sue, and I'll pay her off if I have to."

He pulled out his phone, began typing on it and then looked up at me.

"She's single, and she's thirty years old."

"What's her name?"

"Come on, Grayson, don't." He slowly shook his head.

"What is her name, Julius?"

"Harper Holland."

"Address?"

"Fuck, man. What are you going to do just knock on her door and say, 'Hi honey, I'm your baby daddy?'"

"I'll scope out the situation first."

"Oh, so you're going to stalk the poor woman?"

"No." I rolled my eyes. "Is there a picture of her?"

"No. We don't keep pictures of our customers. Only our donors."

"Then this is what you're going to do for me. You'll send her flowers from the cryobank congratulating her on her pregnancy."

"And how is that going to help?" he asked.

"You'll be the delivery man. And when she opens the door, I'll be able to get a look at her from a distance."

"Are you insane? Have you lost your fucking mind?"

"No. It's simple. So don't make it a big deal. How the hell am I supposed to get to know her if I don't know what she looks like."

"Oh my God." He placed his face in his hands. "You are not seriously going to do this."

"Yes, I am."

"What if she's not home?"

"Then you'll call first. Pretend you're the delivery company and tell her she has a delivery coming and ask if she'll be home to sign for it. You owe me, Julius."

He glared at me as he stood there and shook his head.

"Fine. But if something happens and I go down for this—"

"Nothing will happen. Stop being paranoid. Call me tomorrow when you find out if she's going to be home."

"Whatever, man. I can't believe this. Who the fuck are you?"

"A desperate man trying to keep the company that's rightfully mine."

CHAPTER 10

Harper

I'd spent part of the day contacting several advertising and marketing companies with no luck. I really didn't understand what was going on. I'd never had any trouble securing work and always had a good steady income. I had some leads on website designs which was good, but they didn't pay as well.

I was cleaning up my apartment when my phone rang with a number I didn't recognize.

"Hello."

"Hi, I have a flower delivery for a Miss Harper Holland. I'm about five minutes out and I was wondering if someone will be home to sign for them."

"Yes. I'm home."

"Excellent. I'll see you soon."

Shit. Maybe I shouldn't have told him I was home. My mind started to stir with thoughts that maybe he wasn't a flower delivery guy after all. I'd never had a flower delivery service call me before. I immediately dialed the number he called from.

"Hello."

"This is Harper Holland. Before you deliver the flowers, I need to know who they are from first."

"They're from the New York Cryobank."

"Oh. Okay. Thank you."

I let out a sigh of relief and then there was a knock on the door. Looking out the peephole first, I saw a man in a baseball cap and dark sunglasses standing there holding a large floral arrangement wrapped in paper. I opened the door with a smile.

"Miss Holland?"

"Yes."

"These are for you. I just need you to sign for them."

"I took the piece of paper and pen from him and scribbled my signature.

"There you go." I handed it back to him.

"And here are your flowers." He smiled.

"Thank you."

"Have a nice day and enjoy your flowers." He nodded.

"Thanks. I will."

Grayson

I stood around the corner of the hallway and gulped the moment she opened the door. I honestly didn't know what to expect her to look like, but I knew damn sure I wasn't expecting what I saw. The moment she shut the door, Julius turned and walked down the hallway.

"Let's get out of here. I can't believe you made me do this!" he said.

"She's beautiful," I spoke. "At least from what I could tell from a distance."

"Trust me, bro. She's smoking hot. Damn. I wasn't expecting that," Julius said.

"I wasn't either. Now that I know what she looks like, it's time to put my plan in motion."

"Leave me out of it, Grayson. I've already done too much."

"Don't worry." I hooked my arm around him. "Your work here is done." I smiled.

Harper

I took the wrapping off the flowers to reveal a beautiful arrangement of white and yellow roses. Taking the card, I pulled it from the small envelope and read it.

You have a baby on the way, hooray! Congratulations. We wish you the best of luck and a happy and healthy pregnancy.
Your friends from the New York Cryobank.

These flowers were exactly what I needed to brighten my not so bright day. I sighed as I moved the flowers to the center of my dining table.

The next morning, I grabbed my laptop and headed down the street to Starbucks for a decaf coffee and a cranberry muffin.

"Good morning. What can I get for you?" the barista asked.

"I'll have a Grande decaf coffee and a cranberry muffin."

"Are those any good?" I heard a voice ask behind me.

Turning around, my eyes stared at the sexy man staring back at me with a smile on his face.

"Yes. They're very good." I smiled back.

"It looks like you took the last one," he said.

"Yeah. That's the last one," the barista spoke.

"How would you feel about sharing that with me?"

"Excuse me?" I let out a light laugh.

"I'll have a Grande Americano and put her coffee and muffin on my total," he spoke to the barista.

"I can't let you do that."

"Of course you can." He grinned as he pulled a twenty-dollar bill out of his wallet and handed it to the barista. "Keep the change." He gave her a wink.

"Names?" she asked as she grabbed two cups.

"Grayson. And you are?" The corners of his mouth curved upward as he looked at me.

"Harper."

"It's nice to meet you, Harper." He extended his hand.

"And you as well, Grayson."

My heart skipped a beat as I placed my hand in his. The tailored black designer suit he wore fit his six-foot two-inch stature to perfection. His stylish brown hair, piercing blue eyes and masculine jawline that sported a neatly trimmed five o'clock shadow made my belly flutter. The barista handed me the bag with the muffin in it and my decaf coffee.

"Why don't you go get us a table while I wait for my Americano."

"Sure." I nervously smiled.

I took the muffin, my coffee and my laptop and grabbed us a table by the window. I couldn't believe I was about to share my cranberry muffin with this hot and sexy stranger. Taking the muffin out of the bag, I set down two napkins, cut the muffin in half, and slid it across the table. Grayson finally got his Americano and took a seat.

"Do you always share a muffin with a stranger in Starbucks?" I smirked.

"No. I've never done this before." He gave me a wink, and I gulped. "So, are you here to do some work?" he asked as he pointed to my laptop.

"Yeah." I took a bite of my muffin.

"What type of work do you do?"

"I'm a freelance graphic designer. I'm trying to find new clients. I just lost one of my biggest accounts. The company isn't doing well, and they had to cut costs. How do you like the muffin?"

"It's excellent." He grinned. "Thank you for sharing it with me."

"Thank you for the coffee." I smiled as I held up my cup.

"Do you believe in fate, Harper?" he asked.

"Is that some kind of cheesy pickup line?" I laughed.

He cocked his head and stared at me for a moment.

"Shit. I guess it could be. But it's not a pickup line. My company is looking to hire a graphic designer."

"Really? What company do you work for?"

"Rhodes Enterprises. We're a venture capitalist and property development company. Are you interested?" A smirk crossed his lips. "We pay higher than any other company and the benefits are great."

"So is this position full-time? Like full-time in an office setting?"

"That can be negotiated. Why don't you come in this afternoon for a proper interview? Bring your resume and portfolio, have a look around the office and then we can discuss all the details."

"And what are you going to tell your boss? That you met some random stranger in Starbucks, shared a cranberry muffin, and now she's coming in for an interview?"

He chuckled. "Harper, I am the boss. My last name is Rhodes. My grandfather, Leon Rhodes, started the company fifty years ago. He's retiring in a year and I'll be taking over. The company will become mine."

"Oh." My eyes widened.

He reached in his suit coat pocket and pulled out a business card.

"Here's the address. Will two o'clock work for you?" He grinned as he stood up from his chair.

"Two o'clock is good. I'll see you then." I bit down on my bottom lip.

CHAPTER 11

Harper

I watched him as he walked out of Starbucks. My heart was racing a mile a minute and I couldn't believe what just happened. Looking at my watch, it was nine fifteen, so I grabbed my laptop and my coffee and headed to the upscale salon where Charlotte worked.

"Hey, Harper." Andrea, the receptionist smiled as I walked through the door.

"Hi, Andrea. Is Charlotte with a client?"

"No. Her first client doesn't come in until ten. She's back there if you want to talk to her."

"Thanks."

I walked over to her station and found her sitting in her chair looking at her phone.

"Harper? What are you doing here?" she asked with a smile as she got up and hugged me.

"You will never believe what just happened to me at Starbucks."

"What? Tell me."

"I met this totally hot and sexy guy named Grayson Rhodes. We shared a cranberry muffin and now I'm going to his office at two o'clock for a job interview."

"Wait. What?" She shook her head. "What do you mean you 'shared' a cranberry muffin?"

"I took the last one, and he wanted to try it, so he asked me if I'd share it with him and he bought me the muffin and a coffee. But that's not important." I waved my hand. "His grandfather owns Rhode Enterprises, and he's retiring in a year and Grayson will take over. They're a property development and venture capitalist company, and they're looking for a graphic designer."

"And all this went down at Starbucks?"

"Yes."

"I thought you didn't want to work in an office setting?"

"I don't think I have a choice right now. I need a job with a steady income. When I planned to go ahead with this pregnancy, I didn't think I'd be losing my biggest account. And that's another issue. I'll have to tell him I'm pregnant."

"You're right. You have to. But if he's already impressed with you, I'm sure your pregnancy won't be an issue. How hot and sexy is this guy?" She grinned.

"Ugh. He's tall, brown hair, piercing blue eyes, and he has an amazing body from what I could tell. He's gorgeous."

"How old is he?"

"I'm not sure. I'd say around our age."

"Sounds to me like you're a little smitten with him." She smirked.

"Well, I don't know him." I blushed. "But as far as looks go, I guess you could say that. But it doesn't matter, anyway. I'm pregnant and there's no room in my life for a man. No matter how attracted I am to him."

Grayson

I made Damon park across the street from her building. I didn't know if she was going out this morning or what. It was a chance I took. When I saw her step out the door and walk down the street, I climbed out of the Escalade and followed behind her, blending in with the crowd of people who were on their way to work. She was even more beautiful up close. She stood about five foot seven with long wavy light brown hair. When she turned around and her baby blue eyes stared into mine, they captivated me. She seemed nice and I couldn't for the life of me figure out why the hell she wanted a kid at her age or the fact that she was single. How was a woman that beautiful not spoken for?

On my way into my office, I stopped at Christine's desk.

"Good morning, Mr. Rhodes."

"Good morning, Christine. A woman named Harper Holland is coming in for an interview at two o'clock. If I have anything going on, reschedule it."

"Okay. An interview? I didn't know there was an opening available."

"There wasn't until about thirty minutes ago." I smirked. "I want you to call Lawrence down in Human Resources and ask him to come up."

Walking into my office, I set my briefcase down, took a seat in my chair and stared out at the busy city while I thought about her.

"You wanted to see me, Grayson?"

"Lawrence, yes. Have a seat." I gestured as I turned my chair around. "I'm hiring a graphic designer this afternoon and I want you to get the paperwork ready."

"We don't have an opening for a graphic designer," he said as his brows furrowed.

"We do now. Her name is Harper Holland, and she's coming in at two o'clock. She is to get the full-time benefits package."

"Is she going to be full time?" he asked.

"Probably not but it doesn't matter. She's to have the full-time package. Do you understand me?" I arched my brow at him.

"Yes, I understand, Grayson. I'm not sure what you're doing or why."

"Let's just say I'm in a hospitable mood today." The corners of my mouth curved upward.

CHAPTER 12

Harper

I took a cab to the address on the card that Grayson gave me. As I stepped into the building and took the elevator up to the fifteenth floor, the fluttering in my belly intensified. I was nervous as hell and I shouldn't have been. We'd already had coffee and shared a muffin this morning. I believed it was the fact that I had to tell him I was pregnant. That could be a total game changer for him, and I needed this job.

The elevator doors opened, and when I stepped out, I saw Grayson standing at the front desk.

"Hello, Mr. Rhodes."

"Harper." He turned around with a smile. "Right on time." He looked at his watch. "Follow me and we'll go to my office. May I get you anything? Coffee, tea, water?"

"No, thank you. I'm good."

We stepped into his office and he shut the door.

"Please, have a seat." He gestured as he took the seat behind his desk.

"Here is my resume and portfolio."

He took it from my hands and studied them. I sat there, my hands sweating and my heart racing as I bit down on my bottom lip.

"I see you graduated from NYU with honors. Impressive." He smiled as he looked up at me. "Your portfolio is outstanding. You're very good at what you do. What are these?" he asked as he turned to the back pages of my portfolio.

"Just some buildings I designed. I thought I took those out."

"Are you an architect as well?"

"My major was graphic design, and my minor was architecture."

"These designs are great. Am I to assume you don't like architecture?"

"No. I do. It's just I like graphic design better."

"I see. Well, you've impressed me." He smirked. "You're not interested in working full time in an office setting, are you?"

"Not really. I do much better work on my own in my own space."

"Okay then. How about you come to work for me here at the office two days a week and do the rest of the work at home?"

"Really?" I smiled.

"Yes. Really. But you need to be available if I need you to come in for something and it's not your scheduled day to be here. Will that be a problem?"

"No. Not at all. Except, there's something that I need to tell you first."

"What is it?" He looked at me as he folded his hands.

"I'm pregnant," I nervously spoke.

"I see. I don't have a problem with that. We have a great maternity leave package. Let me ask you though, how far along are you? You certainly don't look pregnant."

"I'm almost eight weeks."

"You and your husband must be thrilled."

"I'm not married." I looked down.

"Oh. Then you and your boyfriend must be thrilled."

"The father isn't in the picture nor will he ever be."

"I see. Your pregnancy doesn't change the fact that I would like you to come work for us." He picked up a pen and wrote something on a piece of paper. "This is the starting salary and you will receive full benefits. Health care, dental, eye care and 401k if you're interested."

I looked at the paper and couldn't believe the figure he wrote. This job would change everything for me.

"This is a very generous offer, Mr. Rhodes."

"Call me Grayson, and we're a generous company." He smiled. "Will you accept the position?"

"Yes. I will definitely accept." I grinned.

"Excellent. Welcome to Rhodes Enterprises, Harper." He stood up and held out his hand. "Come in tomorrow morning at nine a.m. and I'll walk you around and introduce you to everyone and show you your office for the couple days a week you're here."

"Thank you, Grayson. I appreciate you giving me this opportunity."

"You're welcome." The corners of his mouth curved upward. "Enjoy the rest of your day."

"I definitely will. I'm off to apartment hunt."

"Why?" he asked.

"I live in a one bedroom and now with the baby on the way, I need a two-bedroom place."

"Hold on a second." He held up his finger while picking up his phone. "Thomas, it's Grayson Rhodes. Are there any two bedrooms available? Excellent. I'm sending someone over now to have a look. Her name is Harper Holland, and she's an employee of mine. Show her what's available."

He ended the call, picked up his pen, and wrote the address on a piece of paper.

"Ask for Thomas when you get there." He smiled.

"Thank you, Grayson," I spoke as I looked at the address.

I walked out of the building with a smile on my face and hailed a cab. I couldn't believe how everything was just falling into place.

"Where to, lady?" the cab driver asked.

"250 West 50th Street, please."

When the cab driver pulled up to the curb, I climbed out and looked up at the forty-story building. With a smile, I walked through the open door that the doorman held open for me.

"Thank you."

"You're welcome, ma'am. Are you visiting someone?" he asked.

"I'm here to meet with Thomas. Grayson Rhodes sent me over to look at a couple of apartments available for rent."

"Well then, welcome. I'll let Mr. Burns know you're here."

"No need, Sammy." An older gentleman walked over and extended his hand. "You must be Harper. It's nice to meet you."

"And you as well." I placed my hand in his and lightly shook it.

"I have the perfect apartment that I just know you'll love."

I followed him into the elevator, and we took it up to the twentieth floor. Inserting the key into the lock, he opened the door and we stepped inside. My eyes widened at the large space.

"You have eleven hundred and twenty square feet of pure bliss with two bedrooms and two bathrooms," he spoke.

Shit. There was no way I would be able to afford this. Even with this new job.

The walls were painted a light gray with a matching gray wood floor throughout. The modern style kitchen housed white cabinets with granite countertops and stainless-steel appliances. The one thing that caught my attention was the fact that there was a large terrace off the living area. A place I could go sit out at night and enjoy the view of the city.

"And here, behind this door is the washer and dryer. There are only a few apartments in this building that have this included. The rest of the residents have to use our on-site laundry facilities. As you can see, the lighting in here is phenomenal. Because this is an end unit, there are more windows. You're loving it, right?" He grinned.

"I love it. It's perfect. But I'm afraid it might be out of my budget range. What is the rent?"

"You're in luck. We're running a two-year special of five thousand dollars a month including water, sewer and trash removal."

"You're kidding, right? Five thousand a month for this?"

"It's a steal. I can hardly believe it myself. And I do have other people who are interested. But since you're an employee of Mr. Rhodes and he personally sent you himself, the apartment is yours if you want it. And another thing, we're waiving the first and last month's rent. All you must put down is a security deposit of five hundred dollars."

I stood there in disbelief. A place of this size in this area was at the very least over seven thousand if not eight thousand a month.

"I'll take it!" I grinned.

"Perfect. Let's go down to my office and get the paperwork started. You'll be able to move in this weekend if that works for you."

CHAPTER 13

Grayson

As Julius and I were walking into the restaurant, my phone rang. Pulling it from my pocket, I answered it.

"Grayson Rhodes."

"Mr. Rhodes, It's Thomas."

"Hello, Thomas. How did it go with Harper?"

"It went well, sir. She's taking the apartment. She was quite shocked at the monthly rent."

"I'm sure she was. There was no way she'd be able to afford what it really costs with a baby on the way. Thanks for doing this, Thomas."

"You're welcome, sir. Enjoy the rest of your evening."

"What the hell was that all about? What did you do?" Julius asked as he narrowed his eye at me.

Taking a seat at the table, we ordered our drinks and looked over the menu.

"I hired Harper today to work for me and she mentioned that she needed to look for a two-bedroom apartment, so I sent her to one of my buildings in Midtown with a reduce in rent, of course."

He sat across from me and slowly shook his head.

"Are you crazy?"

"No. The first step is getting her to trust me. That woman and her baby are the key to my future."

"You mean YOUR baby," he spoke deadpan. "And how the hell are you going to pull this off?"

"Easy. We'll date, she'll fall in love and when the time is right, I'll tell her about the situation with my grandfather. Now that I've helped her out, she owes me."

"So you're basically going to fuck with her life and emotions. Are you going to tell her it was your sperm she bought?"

"No. God no. There's no way I'm telling her that. Once I convince my grandfather I'm in love with Harper and we're going to be a family, he'll sign over the company to me and then Harper and I will part ways. Once the papers are signed, and the company is mine, there's nothing my grandfather can do."

"You hired her to work for your company. What are you going to do? Fire her once you're done with her?"

"I haven't thought that far ahead yet. Regardless of what happens with our working situation, she'll be well taken care of financially. I'll see to that."

"You've been my best friend forever and I'm sitting here across from you and I feel like I'm talking to a complete stranger."

"Stop being a drama queen, Julius." I sighed. "Everything will work out."

"For you it will and at the expense of Harper Holland."

The next morning as I was walking from the break room to my office, I saw Harper standing by Christine's desk talking to her.

"Good morning." A grin crossed my lips.

"Good morning."

"Let's go in my office. Would you like some coffee?" I asked.

"I'm good. Thank you."

"Did you have a chance to go look at those apartments yesterday?"

"I did and I move in on Saturday."

"Excellent news. I think you'll be very happy there. I'll show you around the office and your workspace and then I'll let you go. I'm sure you have a lot of packing to do."

"I do. I really didn't expect to be moving so quickly." She lightly smiled.

"The next few days are going to be busy for you. So, after the tour, you'll officially start work here on Monday morning."

"Sounds good. Thank you."

I showed her around the office, introduced her to some of the staff and then took her to a small office which would become her workspace for the couple of days she'd be here. I needed to get to know her, but it was too soon to ask her to dinner. I needed to execute the rest of my plan with precision.

CHAPTER 14

Harper

"Oh, my God. Look at this place," Charlotte spoke as she stepped inside my new apartment.

"Shit, Harper. This is so nice," Laurel spoke as she set a box on the floor.

After the movers set all my furniture in the proper place, I stood and looked at the scattered boxes sitting on the floor. After getting the kitchen set up, both Laurel and Charlotte had to leave. Charlotte had to go into the salon to do a bridal party's hair and Laurel had to leave for the airport for a last-minute business trip to Florida.

"I'll be back tomorrow to help you put everything else away. Don't you dare overdo it," Charlotte spoke as she hugged me.

"I won't." I smiled. "I'll see you tomorrow."

Taking in a deep breath, I knew I couldn't rest until I unpacked a few more boxes. The one thing that bothered me was the fact that I needed to find someone to hang my TV on the wall. Maybe maintenance would do it for me. Walking down to the lobby to talk to Sammy, the doorman, my heart nearly stopped when I saw Grayson walk through the doors.

"Grayson." I smiled as I walked over to him.

"Harper. Hi." The corners of his mouth curved upward. "I completely forgot you were moving in today."

"What are you doing here?"

"I was passing by and I thought I'd see if Thomas was in. I need to discuss a business matter with him."

"I'm sorry, Mr. Rhodes. Thomas isn't in today," Sammy spoke.

"Thank you, Sammy. I'll get in touch with him on Monday. So, are you all moved in?"

"Pretty much. I just have a lot of boxes to unpack," I spoke. "I was coming down to see if maintenance could hang my TV on the wall for me."

"I can do that for you." He smiled.

"I couldn't ask you to do that, Grayson," I bashfully spoke.

"You don't have to ask. But I'm doing it, anyway. Lead the way." The grin on his face widened.

We stepped into the elevator and took it up to my apartment.

"Excuse the mess," I said as we stepped inside. "The TV is going on this wall."

"Do you have any tools?" He smirked.

"I have a screwdriver and a hammer." I bit down on my bottom lip.

He let out a chuckle and pulled out his phone.

"This is Grayson Rhodes. I need you to send maintenance up to apartment 2010 immediately."

I stood there and stared at him in his casual tan pants and white button up shirt as he exercised his authority. God, he was so handsome.

Within minutes, maintenance was at my door.

"Thanks for coming up so quickly," Grayson spoke. "The TV is going on this wall."

"Sure thing, Mr. Rhodes." One of the maintenance men smiled.

"You sure know how to get things done." I glanced at him as he stood next to me.

"It's easy when you're the boss." He winked.

Once they put the TV on the wall, and it was all hooked up, Grayson reached in his pocket and tipped the maintenance men.

"Thank you. If at any time Miss Holland calls, I want you up here attending to whatever it is she needs. Understood?"

"Of course, Mr. Rhodes." Both men smiled before walking out the door.

"Thank you, Grayson. I really appreciate it."

"You're welcome. I should get going. It looks like you have a lot to do."

He walked over to the door, placed his hand on the handle and then turned to me.

"Would you like to join me for dinner tonight?" he asked.

I took in a deep breath as the butterflies in my belly started to flutter.

"I'd love to." A smile crossed my lips.

"I'll pick you up at seven." The corners of his mouth curved upward.

"I'll be ready."

The moment the door shut I let out a deep breath. My head was spinning with happiness, and for the first time in a very long time, I felt alive. He knew I was pregnant but yet he still wanted to take me out. Maybe I was imagining things. No. He was definitely flirting with me.

I had just finished changing my clothes, and as I was running a brush through my long brown hair, there was a knock at the door. Looking at the clock, it was only six thirty. There was no way he was thirty minutes early. Walking to the door, I opened it and saw Charlotte standing there.

"Charlotte? What are you doing here? I thought you had a date tonight?"

"The douchebag cancelled." She pushed past me. "I decided to come over and help you." She stood there and stared at me with a narrowing eye. "Why are you dressed up?"

"Actually," I smiled, "I have dinner plans with someone."

"And who is this someone?" She placed her hand on her hip.

"Grayson Rhodes. He's picking me up at seven."

"Your boss, Grayson Rhodes?"

"Yes." I grinned. "I saw him in the lobby earlier. He came up and had maintenance hang my TV and then he asked me to join him for dinner."

"Harper, he's your boss. Do you think it's a good idea?"

"It's only dinner, Char."

"Okay." She bit down on her bottom lip. "Remember the only thing you need to think about right now is that baby growing inside of you."

"Exactly. So I better get out and have some fun while I can." I gave her a wink.

She took a seat on the couch and put her feet up on the coffee table.

"Well, just so you know, I'm sticking around. I want to meet this Grayson Rhodes for myself."

I sighed as I rolled my eyes and walked into the bedroom. Taking one last look at myself in the mirror and slipping into my shoes, I heard a knock. Running out of my room, I ran to the door before Charlotte could open it.

"Go sit back down!" I exclaimed.

I opened the door with a smile when I saw Grayson standing there holding a bouquet of white lilies and yellow roses.

"Hi." The corners of his mouth curved upward.

"Hi." I grinned.

"These are for you. I feel every new home should have fresh flowers."

"Thank you, Grayson. They're beautiful. Come in while I put these in a vase."

The moment he stepped inside, Charlotte walked over to him.

"Hey there. I'm Charlotte. Harper's best friend." She extended her hand.

"Grayson Rhodes. It's nice to meet you, Charlotte."

"Likewise, Mr. Rhodes."

"Thanks for stopping by, Charlotte," I spoke as I filled a vase with water. "I'll see you tomorrow?"

"Yes. I'll be over in the morning with coffee and bagels."

"Sounds good." I smiled at her.

CHAPTER 15

Grayson

"She seems nice," I spoke as I walked over to where Harper was standing and arranging the flowers.

"She's the best."

"What line of work is she in?"

"She's a hairstylist."

"Ah. So is she the one responsible for your beautiful hair?" I smirked.

"Yeah. I guess she is." She bit down on her bottom lip as her cheeks turned pink.

"We should get going. I've made reservations for us at Eleven Madison Park for seven thirty."

"Just let me grab my purse."

We walked down to the lobby and out of the building where Damon was waiting for us at the curb.

"Damon, I would like you to meet Miss Harper Holland. Harper, this is my driver Damon."

"Good evening, Miss Holland. It's very nice to meet you."

"Good evening, Damon." She smiled as I helped her inside the Escalade.

As soon as we arrived at the restaurant, we followed the hostess to a booth that sat in the corner, per my request. It was the quietest spot in the place. Upon sitting down, we both picked up our menus and looked them over.

"Good evening, Mr. Rhodes. It's good to see you again."

"Good evening, Ramone."

"May I bring you a bottle of our finest wine?" he asked.

"Not tonight. I'll have a bourbon and my guest will have—"

"Just water, please," Harper spoke.

"Sparkling?" Ramone smiled at her.

"That'll be fine. Thank you."

After Ramone brought us our drinks, we placed our dinner order. I couldn't help but stare at her. She was beautiful, and I was desperate to find out all about her.

"So, Harper Holland," I smiled. "Have you lived in New York your whole life?"

She picked up her glass and took a sip of her water.

"No. I moved here when I was eighteen and attended NYU."

"And you never left?"

"There was no reason for me to. I'd already spent four years here and made friends, so I stayed and created a new life for myself."

"What about your family?"

"If you're referring to my parents, they were killed in an automobile accident back in Florida when I was nine. The only other living relative I have is my Aunt Nicole. After my parents died, I was sent to Virginia to live with her."

"I'm sorry."

"Thank you. That was a long time ago. I didn't want to be there as much as she didn't want me there. She was a waitress and an alcoholic. I pretty much raised myself. I figured out at an early age that if I ever wanted to get out of that godforsaken town, I'd have to get a good scholarship. So, I buried myself in my schoolwork, got straight A's, volunteered as much as I could, graduated as the valedictorian of my graduating class and received a full ride to NYU. The day after I graduated high school, I packed my bags and never looked back."

THE DONOR

"You're a very smart woman. Sounds to me like you were very responsible at such a young age."

"I had no choice. The day my parents died, I lost my childhood. I had to grow up quickly. I guess taking care of an alcoholic aunt will do that to you."

"Do you still keep in touch with her?"

"No. I haven't spoken to her since the day I left." She looked down and ran her finger around the rim of her glass.

"It's probably for the best. She sounds like a very toxic person."

"She was." Her lips gave way to a light smile. "How about you, Mr. Rhodes? What's your story?"

I picked up my bourbon and brought it to my lips.

"Like you, I lost my parents at a young age when their private jet crashed. So my grandparents raised me. When I was sixteen, my grandmother passed away from cancer, so it was just me and my grandfather. I graduated high school and went off to Yale to get my MBA. Then I came to work for my grandfather."

"I'm sorry about your parents."

"Thanks. But like you said, it was a long time ago."

We finished our dinner and then I took her home.

"Is it okay if I walk you up to your apartment?" I asked.

"I'd like that." She bashfully smiled.

She stuck her key in the lock and opened the door. Flipping the light switch, she set down her purse and walked over to the window.

"Wow. I don't think I'll ever grow tired of this amazing view at night."

"It is spectacular. I'm happy you like the apartment," I said as I stood next to her.

"Thank you, Grayson." She turned and our eyes locked.

Bringing the back of my hand up to her cheek, I softly stroked it.

"You're welcome. And thank you for keeping me company tonight. I had a nice time."

"So did I." A smile crossed her lips.

I wanted to kiss her, but it was too soon. Actually, I wanted more than a kiss and I knew if I didn't leave, I'd regret it.

"Enjoy your day tomorrow," I spoke as I stroked her cheek one last time.

"You too."

Placing my hand in my pocket, I opened the door and walked out. When I climbed into the car, Damon looked at me through the rearview mirror.

"Harper seems like a very nice woman."

"She is."

"I'm not sure I've ever met someone like her before."

"What's that supposed to mean?" I asked.

"It's just the company of women you keep are different. What are you up to, Grayson?"

I sighed as I looked out the window and ignored him.

CHAPTER 16

Harper

I placed my hand on my cheek where Grayson touched it. I swore I could still feel his hand on it. The softness of his touch aroused me, and I desperately begged in silence for his lips to touch mine. Instead, he was a perfect gentleman who was in complete control of his actions.

As I climbed into bed, my phone dinged with a text message from him.

"I just wanted to say goodnight. Sweet dreams."

"Goodnight, Grayson."

When I awoke the next morning, I felt like I was on cloud nine, except for the nausea that settled in my belly. Climbing out of bed, I went into the bathroom where I washed my face and brushed my teeth before Charlotte came by. I sighed as I walked into the living room and stared at the rest of the boxes that needed unpacking. It would be a long day.

Ten o'clock rolled around when Charlotte knocked on my door. Opening it, she stood there holding up a brown bag and a cup holder with two coffee cups sitting inside.

"One decaf for you, one fuel for me and a variety of bagels with two different cream cheeses." She grinned as she pushed past me and went into the kitchen. "I want to hear all about your night with Grayson Rhodes," she spoke as she opened the cabinet and took down two small plates.

"Dinner was amazing." I smiled. "In fact, he's amazing."

I grabbed our coffees and took them to the table.

"You're in trouble," she said as she set the bagels in the center of the table.

"Why?" My brows furrowed.

"Because you're falling for him and you barely know him." She pointed her knife at me. "Did you google him yet?"

"No. I don't think there's a need to. He's genuinely a nice guy."

"Who are you?" She shook her head. "You don't trust men at all. Especially after Kevin. You went into hiding for a year, decided to have a child on your own and now all of a sudden, this man whom you've known like two days is suddenly the best thing in the world? I'm worried about you, Harper. I don't want to see you get hurt again. Things are different now."

I sighed as I took a bite of my bagel.

"You're trusting way too fast," she said. "Listen, I love you. But your hormones are all over the place right now. All I'm saying is just be careful. A high-powered man like Grayson Rhodes doesn't seem like the family type of guy. Did you know that he's number one on the New York's most eligible bachelor's list?"

"And how do you know that?"

"I googled him last night."

"Of course you did. I'm done talking about this. Let's get these boxes unpacked," I spoke with irritation as I got up from the table.

"Don't be mad at me. I'm just asking you to be careful. Sometimes people aren't who they seem. You of all people know that."

Maybe Charlotte was right and what I was feeling were my hormones way out of control. I had a hard time trusting men, so why was I so quick to trust Grayson?

THE DONOR

The next morning, I got up early, got dressed and headed down to the lobby of my building.

"Good morning, Miss Holland." Sammy smiled.

"Good morning, Sammy. Please, just call me Harper."

"Can I get a cab for you?"

"That would be great. Thank you. Today is my first day at the office. I'll only be working there two days a week and then working from home the rest of the time."

"Sounds like the perfect schedule." He smiled as a cab pulled up to the curb. "Have a great day, Harper."

"Thanks, Sammy. You too."

I walked into the building and took the elevator up to my small office. As I was putting my purse away, I heard a voice from the doorway.

"Good morning."

I turned around and smiled when I saw Grayson and another man standing there.

"Good morning."

"I trust you got your apartment in order yesterday."

"I did." I grinned.

"Excellent." The corners of his mouth curved upward. "Harper, I'd like you to meet, Curtis. Curtis, Harper Holland."

"It's wonderful to meet you." He greeted me with a wide grin as he extended his hand.

"It's nice to meet you too, Curtis."

"Curtis is going to be your partner so to speak while you're here in the office. He'll show you around and any questions you have, he can help you."

Curtis was a man in his early forties. He stood about five foot ten with spikey blond hair, a clean-shaven face and bright green eyes. Too bright to be natural. I suspected he was wearing colored contacts.

"I have a meeting to get to. We'll talk later." He gave me a wink before walking out of my office.

My insides fluttered at the sight of him. It wasn't only how he looked in his designer suits or the way he kept himself perfectly groomed. It was the confidence he exuded. I needed to focus on my job and not Grayson Rhodes.

"Don't take this the wrong way, Harper, but I'm really shocked that Grayson is letting you work here only two days a week and the rest at home. He's never done that before and I'm afraid it might cause some problems with the other employees. Especially the ones who wanted to cut back to part time, and he told them no. He said if they couldn't fulfill the full-time hours here, then they needed to quit."

"Shit. Really?" I bit down on my bottom lip. "Maybe he's changing and he's starting with me?"

"I doubt it. He must have some ulterior motive as to why he's letting you split your time. There's a motive behind everything he does."

As I stood there and listened to him, I got the impression Curtis wasn't too fond of Grayson. The last thing I needed were the other employees hating me because of my work schedule. That was why I never liked working in an office setting. Between the backstabbing, gossiping and assumptions, it was draining. Not to mention that you couldn't trust anyone even if you thought they were your friend. That was a hassle I didn't need in my life and why I did freelance work on my time from home. Away from all the office politics and bullshit. Two days a week at the office wouldn't be so bad. It wasn't like I really had a choice. I needed to make sure that my baby would be taken care of and I would sacrifice everything to make sure that happened.

CHAPTER 17

Grayson

My meeting ran longer than I thought it would. I stopped by Harper's office and found her sitting behind her desk staring at her computer.

"Well? How are things going so far?"

"Great." She smiled. "How was your meeting?"

"It was long but good. That's why I stopped by." I glanced at my watch. "I'm starving. Have you had lunch yet?"

"No. Not yet."

"Then grab your purse and let's go." I grinned. "You need to feed that baby. We can talk business over lunch. There's a diner a couple blocks over that have the best Rueben sandwiches."

"Sounds good." A smile crossed her lips as she grabbed her purse and we headed out of the office.

We were seated at a booth looking over the menu when Harley, the perky redhead approached the table with a flirty grin across her lips.

"Hey, Grayson. Long time no see."

"Hello, Harley. My secretary has been picking up my orders. Busy times at the office."

"It's good to see you. Still looking as handsome as ever. What can I start you off with?"

"Harper?"

"Just water for me."

"And for me as well. I think we're ready to order. I'll have the Rueben sandwich."

"And I'll have the same." She smiled as she closed the menu and handed it to her.

"Two Reubens coming right up."

The moment she walked away, Harper stared at me.

"Looking as handsome as ever?"

"She loves to flirt. What can I say?" I smirked. "There's something I want to talk to you about."

"Okay. I'm listening."

"The meeting I was in earlier, it had to do with a piece of property I purchased. We're bulldozing the building that's already there and building brand-new high-rise apartments. I want you to design the building."

"Me?" She pointed to herself. "You want me to design the building?"

"Yes. Now I know graphic design is your thing but from what I saw in the back of your portfolio you're a damn good architect too."

"You're not giving me a choice, are you?"

"No."

"Then I'm excited to get started on my first project." She smiled.

Her smile was infectious, and one couldn't help but smile back at her. I noticed it in the office, and I noticed it when we were out.

Harley walked over with two plates in her hand.

"For you," she spoke as she set down Harper's plate first. "And for you handsome." She winked at me.

"Thanks, doll." I flirtatiously smiled at her.

Harper picked up her sandwich and bit into it.

"Oh my God! You weren't kidding. This is amazing."

"I told you. One of the best Reubens in New York City."

I sat across from her and watched as she enjoyed her sandwich.

She had a glow. An inner peace that I could feel radiating from her. The more time I spent with her, the more I wanted to fuck her. To feel the warmth of her all over my cock. I could only imagine what it felt like to be buried deep inside her. Skin to skin. No condom needed since she was already pregnant. No worries, no care. She had a piece of sauerkraut hanging from the corner of her mouth, so I reached across the table and softly wiped it away with my thumb.

"You had a piece of sauerkraut."

She picked up her napkin and wiped her mouth as her pink colored cheeks became more prominent. She was blushing, and it was cute.

"Thank you."

I gave her a smile as I picked up my sandwich and finished it.

As soon as we arrived back to the office, my phone rang. Pulling it from my pocket, I saw my grandfather was calling.

"Grandfather. To what do I owe the pleasure?"

"I'm leaving for Santa Barbara tomorrow and I was hoping we could have dinner tonight."

"Of course, where?"

"Daniel at seven o'clock."

"I'll be there."

Ending the call, I sighed as I placed my phone in my pocket. Tonight would be the perfect night to tell him about Harper so he could get that ridiculous notion out of his head about handing the company over to Alfie.

I stayed at the office until it was time to leave to meet my grandfather. Climbing out of the Escalade, I told Damon I'd catch a cab home and that he could leave for the night.

"Enjoy your dinner, Grayson."

"With any luck, it'll be the best dinner of my life." I grinned as I shut the door.

Walking inside the restaurant the hostess walked me over to where my grandfather sat.

"Hello, Grayson." He nodded.

"Hello, Grandfather."

"Good evening, Mr. Rhodes. May I start you off with a drink?"

"Yes, Carlos, I'll have a bourbon. Make it a double."

"Long day?" my grandfather asked as he sipped his scotch.

"It was. The deal is closed on the Park Avenue property. We bulldoze the building next week."

"Excellent. And the plans for the new high-rise are ready?"

"Not yet. But they are being worked on."

"I haven't been hearing anything about you lately. Have you been behaving yourself?"

"Actually," I smiled as Carlos set down my drink, "I've met someone."

He sat there and steadily narrowed his eye at me like he always did when he needed to decide if he believed me or not.

"Interesting and quite quickly may I add. Remember what I told you, Grayson, about trying to pull a fast one on me."

"I can promise you that I didn't meet her because of what you told me. I actually met her standing in line at Starbucks. Her name is Harper Holland. We got to talking and it just so happened she was looking for a job. She's a graphic design artist and we were in need of one."

"I don't recall needing another graphic artist." His brow furrowed.

"We did. I brought her in for an interview and not only is she good with graphic arts, she's a phenomenal architect designer. You should have seen the buildings and houses she designed."

"I see. Are the two of you seeing each other?"

"I've taken her to lunch and dinner and I'm hoping to see a lot more of her. There's something about her, Grandfather." I smiled. "I can't explain it. I feel different when I'm around her and I want to know everything about her."

"I want to meet the woman who has captured my grandson's heart." He finished off his drink.

"You will as soon as you get back from your trip. We'll all go to dinner.

"You do know, Grayson, that it's not wise to mix business with pleasure."

"I know, but this can't be helped. I really like this woman. For the first time in a very long time, I actually want to spend my time with someone."

"Does this Harper feel the same way about you?"

"I think she does." I grinned. "She's the one I'm having design the high rise."

"Why? We have a company who designs our buildings."

"Why not? She's good and we can save time and money by having it done in-house."

Carlos walked over and before he could set my grandfather's drink down, he took it from his hands and held it up.

"Here's to the start of a beautiful relationship." He winked, and I tipped my glass to his.

Once dinner was over and we said our goodbyes, I climbed into the back of a cab and headed home. Convincing my grandfather that I was interested in Harper was easy. But then again, I was always good at convincing him of things. Once I had Harper Holland in the palm of my hand, things would be a lot easier. I wouldn't have to try so hard or feel the need to see her all the time. But for now, I needed to do everything I could to get her to fall in love with me.

CHAPTER 18

*H*arper
When I arrived home from work, I cooked myself dinner and then started a rough draft of the high rise. This building was for the elite; the wealthy. The ones who wouldn't flinch at spending twenty million plus to live there. The pressure was on because I'd never designed anything worth this much. A project like this was meant to be in the hands of a high-powered architect firm, not in the hands of someone like me. I couldn't stop thinking about Grayson and the lunch we had today. The way his thumb gently wiped away the sauerkraut from my mouth was unnerving and every inch of my body trembled. As I was trying to concentrate on designing the building, my phone dinged with a text message from him and instantly a smile crossed my lips.

"Hey there. What are you doing?"

"Hi. I've just started the design for the high-rise. What are you doing?"

"I just got home. I had dinner with my grandfather. He wants to meet you."

"He does?"

"He's leaving on a trip tomorrow, but I told him we'd have dinner when he returns to New York. Is that okay with you?"

"Sure. I'd love to meet him. Why does he want to meet me?"

"Our entire dinner conversation may have revolved around you. I told him what an amazing woman you are."

I could feel the heat rise in my cheeks as I read his message.

"Thank you, Grayson."

"You're welcome and it's true. I think you are amazing, and I was hoping we could have dinner together tomorrow night. That's if you don't already have plans."

"I'd love to have dinner with you. How about we have dinner here? I'll whip us up something really good. Say around six thirty?"

"It's a date. You won't be in the office tomorrow, right?"

"No. Not tomorrow. I'm spending the day here working on the building."

"Then I'll see you tomorrow evening. Looking forward to it."

"Me too."

"You've had a long day and must be tired. Relax for the rest of the evening. The design can wait until tomorrow. Sweet dreams."

"Good night, Grayson."

With a wide grin across my face, I set my phone down and got up to make a cup of tea. Grayson was right. I was tired, and the design could wait until tomorrow when I was refreshed from a good night's sleep. Once the hot water was ready, I poured it into a mug and slipped in a tea bag. Taking it over to the couch, I pulled up the notes in my phone and started planning our dinner for tomorrow night. But first, I had a question for Grayson.

"Do you like Italian food?"

"I love Italian food."

"Good. Then I shall cook Italian tomorrow night."

"You already have my mouth watering."

"You may not like it."

"I'll love it."

"We'll see. Good night."

"Good night."

The next morning, I got up early and headed to the market to pick up everything I needed for dinner before I started my work for the day. I bought more than I could carry, and as soon as Sammy saw me, he opened the door and grabbed a couple of bags from me.

"Here, let me help you with these," he spoke.

"Thanks, Sammy. I honestly didn't intend to get this much."

He followed me in the elevator and up to my apartment. After unlocking the door, we stepped inside and set the bags down in the kitchen. I reached in my wallet and pulled out some cash for a tip.

"No, Harper, I can't accept that."

"Oh, come on, Sammy. I wouldn't have made it up here if it wasn't for your help."

"It was my pleasure to help you." A smile crossed his lips.

I don't know why, but I had this overwhelming need to tell him that I was pregnant. I didn't want him to be shocked when I started showing.

"Thank you, again. I think there's something you should know about me since we talk just about every day."

"What is it?" he asked.

"I'm pregnant, the father isn't in the picture, and I used a sperm donor. Don't judge."

"Congratulations, Harper. What exciting news. I would never judge. I think it's great."

"Thanks. I just wanted to tell you so you're not shocked when I begin to show."

"I'm happy you told me. Enjoy the rest of your day." He smiled as he gave a nod of his head.

I liked Sammy. He was an older gentleman in his late fifties who stood about six feet tall with short salt and pepper hair. He was very kind and there was something about him that made me feel comfortable. In a strange way, he reminded me of my father. Maybe it was his broad shoulders and the way he carried himself.

I worked on the design for the high rise all day, talked to Laurel and Charlotte and then it was time to prep dinner. I wanted nothing more than tonight to be perfect. A perfect dinner with a perfect man.

CHAPTER 19

Grayson

I climbed out of the car and walked through the doors of The Grill where I met Julius for lunch.

"Sorry I'm a few minutes late," I spoke as I slid in the seat across from him. "I got stuck on a conference call."

"No worries, bro."

I picked up the menu and looked it over.

"I think I'm just going to get the lobster salad."

"That's it?" Julius asked.

"Yeah. I don't want to eat too much. Harper is cooking dinner for me tonight."

"So I take it things with her are going as planned?"

"Yes." The corners of my mouth curved upward. "My grandfather wants to meet her after I sang her praises at dinner last night. I have no doubt in my mind that once he meets her, all doubts about signing the company over to me will be gone."

"I'm still not comfortable with this, Grayson. Do you even remotely like her?"

"She's a nice girl and I enjoy spending time with her. But if you're asking if I'm getting emotionally involved, the answer is no. I'm physically attracted to her which is a bonus because it makes my plan a lot easier. The four of us should get together one night."

"And you don't think she'll recognize me? Have you forgotten I'm the one who delivered her flowers?"

"You were in street clothes and dark sunglasses. She won't recognize you."

"I don't know. Like I said I don't want any part of this."

"Too late, bro. You're already in. She's going to think it's weird if I don't introduce her to my friends. You need to play your part. At least until I get my company."

He sat across from me and slowly shook his head.

"Everything is going to work out. Don't worry about it," I said.

"I just don't see how fucking with someone's life and emotions is going to work out."

*

I left the office early to go home, shower and change clothes before heading over to Harper's apartment. On my way there, I had Damon drop me off at the florist so I could pick up a dozen baby pink roses for her.

"Good evening, Mr. Rhodes." Sammy smiled as he held the door open for me.

"Good evening, Sammy."

"Beautiful roses."

"Thank you. They're for Harper. She's having me over for dinner."

"Ah. I helped her earlier with her groceries. She's a great woman."

"She is." I smiled as the elevator doors opened and I stepped inside.

Knocking on the door, I stood there holding the bouquet of roses behind my back.

"Hi." A wide grin graced her face as she opened the door.

"Hi. These are for you." I handed her the bouquet with a smile.

"Grayson, they're beautiful. Thank you. Come in."

The moment I stepped inside, the aroma of a home cooked meal smacked me in the face.

"Wow, Harper. It smells delicious in here."

"Dinner will be ready in a few minutes. Make yourself comfortable."

"What can I do to help?"

"Nothing. Everything is just about done."

She went into the kitchen to place the flowers in a vase and I walked over to the table that was set.

"You didn't have to go to all this trouble," I spoke as I walked into the kitchen.

"It was no trouble at all. I love to cook. You can take the salad over to the table." She handed me the large wooden bowl which held a beautiful-looking antipasto salad.

Walking back to the kitchen, she arranged what looked like stuffed zucchini on a plate.

"What are those?" I asked for they looked and smelled delicious.

"Italian sausage stuffed zucchini." She smiled.

I took the plate of zucchini and the bread she cut up over to the table while she pulled a glass dish out of the oven.

"I hope you like Caprese Chicken," she spoke as she set it down in the center of the table.

"It's one of my favorites."

I took a seat at the table and looked at the meal she cooked for me. Caprese Chicken, Italian sausage stuffed zucchini, antipasto salad and fresh bread.

"Shit. I forgot the wine," she said as she began to get up from her seat.

"Sit down. I'll get it."

"It's on the counter and there's a glass in the cabinet next to the stove. Would you mind grabbing me a bottle of water from the refrigerator?"

"Coming right up." I gave her a wink.

Not only was she a good designer, she was also an excellent cook. I didn't think I'd ever had a home-cooked meal this delicious before.

"Where did you learn to cook like this?" I asked.

"My mother taught me. My aunt never cooked, and if I wanted to eat, I had to do all the cooking. My mom was a huge cook, and she always had me in the kitchen helping her ever since I was about two years old. I learned a lot from her and over the years I found that being in the kitchen was therapeutic for me. It calms my mind down if that makes sense. Plus, there's the creative aspect of it."

"I can understand that," I spoke as I took a bite of the Caprese Chicken. "This is amazing."

I wasn't just telling her that to make her feel good. I genuinely meant it. Everything about this dinner was exceptional. Especially the Italian sausage stuffed zucchini. I'd never had it before, and it was quickly becoming one of my favorite foods.

When we finished dinner, I cleared the table while she started to clean up the kitchen. When I walked in with the dishes in my hand, she was standing over the sink washing the glass dish she cooked the chicken in. Walking up behind her, I placed my hands in the soapy water on top of hers.

"Let me clean this up," I softly spoke in her ear. "You go sit down and relax."

She froze and slightly turned her head.

"Thank you. I got this."

"But I insist." My breath traveled down her neck.

I heard the sharp inhale of her breath as I removed her hands from the water, grabbed a towel and began to dry them off. She turned around in my arms and instantly our eyes locked while I finished drying them off.

"You're my guest," she softly spoke.

The corners of my mouth curved upward as I stared into her beautiful eyes. Removing the towel from her hands, I set it down and placed my finger under her chin.

"I want to," I spoke in a mere whisper as I slowly leaned in and brushed my lips against hers.

To be honest, I didn't know what to expect. Maybe she'd return my kiss, or she'd pull away and slap me. She welcomed my lips and with a slight part, I slipped my tongue inside and met hers for the first time.

CHAPTER 20

Harper

My body was on fire. The softness of his lips against mine was tantalizing as was the warmth of his tongue dancing with mine. His hands moved up and down my body as mine tangled through his hair, and the hardness of his cock pressed against my belly.

"I can stop if you want me to," he whispered as he broke our kiss and placed his hand on my cheek.

"I don't want you to stop."

Instantly, his mouth smashed into mine while he scooped me up and carried me into the bedroom, laying me gently on the bed. He hovered over me, his lips tangling with mine as his hand fondled my breast. He sat me up and lifted my shirt over my head and tossed it on the floor. His eyes diverted to the cleavage that my push up bra so eloquently provided. Reaching around my back, he unhooked my bra and slid it off me.

I lay back down while his mouth traveled to my breasts, softly stroking each one with his tongue before taking my hardened peaks in his mouth. A moan erupted from me.

"Your breasts are so beautiful," he whispered as he cupped one of them in his strong hands while his mouth worked the other.

Before I knew it, he'd unbuttoned my pants and slid them off my hips, taking them off with one smooth pull. He brought his mouth up to mine as his hand slid down the front of my panties and his finger dipped inside me. A louder moan erupted from me as I arched my back in ecstasy. He touched me in ways I'd never been touched before.

"Before I bury myself deep inside you, I want you to come for me."

It wasn't hard to grant his wish as he skillfully explored me. I was at the edge of the cliff and ready to dive off into a beautiful mind-blowing orgasm. The feeling was unreal and unlike anything I'd ever felt before. I'd had plenty of orgasms in my life, but never one as heightening as what I was about to experience. My fingers gripped the comforter as the release happened and I couldn't help but let out noises I didn't even know could come from me.

"Perfect. Absolutely perfect." A smile crossed his lips as he stared into my eyes.

He climbed off the bed and started to strip out of his clothes. He removed his unbuttoned shirt and tossed it to the floor. His body was a gift from the gods. A beautiful ripped, toned and muscular body. I held my breath in anticipation as he unbuttoned his pants and slid them down. I couldn't help but stare at his all black boxer briefs that fit him like a glove. He gripped the sides of his briefs and pulled them down revealing the package I fantasized about since I'd met him. He was blessed, and I was about to be.

"Do you trust me?" he asked.

"I do."

"Enough not to use a condom. You're already pregnant so we don't have to worry about that, and I can guarantee you that I'm one hundred percent clean," he spoke as he hovered over me.

"I trust you."

Reaching up, I placed my hand on the back of his head and pulled his lips to mine. He slowly thrust inside me and I gasped at the feeling that overtook me. Moving in and out of me with precision, I felt intoxicated. Moans escaped both of us as we enjoyed each other, and my body geared up for another orgasm. I howled in delight as my legs tightened around him and a rush of warmth flooded me. His thrusts slowed and suddenly stopped as his cock buried itself deep inside me and exploded. His body collapsed on mine while his hands tangled in my hair and my arms tightened around him. I could feel the rapid beating of his heart and suddenly I knew I was done for.

"Shit," he spoke with bated breath as he rolled off me and laid on his back with his hand over his heart.

I rolled on my side and snuggled into him as his arm wrapped around me and his lips kissed the top of my head.

"Are you okay?" he asked.

"I don't think I've ever been better." I smiled as I lifted my head from his chest and looked at him.

"Can I ask you a personal question? If you don't want to answer it's fine. I'll understand."

"What do you want to know?"

"What happened to the baby's father? Did he not want the baby or something?"

I knew that question would come eventually, and I was fully prepared to answer it. I sat up, grabbed the blanket at the end of the bed and wrapped myself in it as I faced him.

"I chose this pregnancy on my own with the help of a sperm donor."

"I see. Do you personally know the donor?"

"I only know him as Donor 137665."

"You went through a cryobank?" he asked.

"Yes. The only thing I ever wanted was a family. After my parents died, I never had another family. My aunt never wanted me because she was too selfish to ever think about anyone but herself and her alcohol. She was my mom's sister and they hadn't spoken in three years."

"What about your father's side of the family?"

"My father was originally from Germany and left when he was twenty years old. Him and his parents had some kind of falling out and he left and never looked back. He told me that he'd tell me the story when I was old enough to understand, but he never got the opportunity. So, CPS tracked down my aunt and shipped me off to her."

"I'm sorry," he spoke as he grabbed my hand and held it.

"My relationship with men never really seemed to pan out. And as for my last relationship, my fiancé ended it three months before our wedding."

"You were engaged?"

"I was. Then he told me he wasn't sure that he loved me enough to spend the rest of his life with me." I looked down as the words I spoke still hurt.

"What a bastard. But it was better that you found out before you married the asshole."

"I know." I gave a light smile. "So I decided that I was going to raise a child on my own. It wasn't something that I just decided one day when I woke up. I'd given it serious thought for about a year. This baby means the world to me." I placed my hands on my belly.

He stared at me as he ran the back of his hand down my cheek.

"I think you'll make an amazing mother."

"I hope so."

He leaned forward and softly brushed his lips against mine.

"I should get going. It's late."

"You can stay," I spoke with the hopes he'd say yes.

"I need to be at the office early tomorrow. Perhaps another time." The corners of his mouth curved upward as he ran his thumb across my lips.

CHAPTER 21

Grayson

I climbed out of bed and slipped into my clothes. A part of me wanted to stay but I knew I needed to leave.

"Are you coming to the office tomorrow?" I asked her as I sat on the edge of the bed and slipped into my shoes.

"Yes. Mondays and Wednesdays like we agreed."

We both walked out into the living area and I realized we didn't finish cleaning up.

"Shit. We didn't finish cleaning up. I'll help you before I leave."

"No." She placed her hand on my chest. "I can do it. There's not that much."

"Are you sure? I don't mind staying and helping."

"I'm positive. Go and I'll see you in the morning."

She wrapped her arms around my neck, and I brought my lips to hers.

"I'll see you in the morning," I spoke.

I walked down to the lobby and exited the building just as a cab was pulling up to the curb.

"Are you available?" I asked the driver through the window.

"Sure. Get in. Where to?"

"829 Park Avenue."

The moment I got home, I poured myself a bourbon and sat down at my piano. Holding the glass in one hand, I stroked the keys with the other. I'd sealed the deal tonight and had Harper right where I wanted her. I finished my drink and went upstairs to take a shower. The smell of her was all over me and as much as I loved it, I couldn't give anymore thought about what happened between us. I was only in this to get my company. Nothing more. I was sorry for what she went through with her fiancé, but she was pregnant now and getting what she always wanted.

I lay in bed and tossed and turned for a majority of the night. I'd finally fallen asleep when the damn alarm went off. My eyes flew open, and I rolled over and turned it off. I needed to get up and get to the office before Harper did. After all, I told her I couldn't stay the night with her because I needed to be in early. Climbing out of bed, I let out a long yawn and stepped in the cool shower with the hopes it would wake me up. I had Damon make a detour to Starbucks so I could grab a coffee that I desperately needed.

"I take it you didn't sleep well," he spoke.

"Not really."

"Too much Harper Holland on the mind?"

"No. I'll be right back," I said as I climbed out and went inside.

Thankfully, there were only two people ahead of me. Looking over at the glass case, I spotted a cranberry muffin.

"Good morning. What can I get you?" the barista asked.

"A Grande Flat White with three shots of espresso, a Grande dark roast and a cranberry muffin."

"Name for the order?"

"Grayson."

I pulled out my wallet, handed her some cash and waited for my muffin and coffees. I grabbed the bag and drink carrier, climbed in the back of the Escalade and handed Damon his coffee.

"Thank you, Grayson."

"You're welcome. Now tell me why you said what you did earlier about Harper."

"Because you had dinner with her last night and I'm assuming it went well."

"It did. She's an excellent cook."

Damon wasn't stupid. He'd known me for years and he always had my back where my grandfather was concerned. He was the only other person besides Julius that I would trust with my life.

"She almost sounds perfect." He smiled.

"Listen, Damon, you'll be seeing Harper a lot. But I want you to remember that not everything will be as it seems."

"What are you doing, Grayson?" he asked as his eyes darted at me through the rearview mirror.

"My grandfather gave me a year to find someone and fall in love or else he's signing the company over to someone else."

"So you're using her?"

"In a sense, yes. And there's something else you need to know. She's pregnant. She used a sperm donor from the cryobank."

"The one where Julius works at?"

"Yes."

"I see."

"I don't want or need your judgment. I need to do what's best for me and my future. Harper just happened to fall in my lap at the right time."

"There's more to life than a high-powered company and money, Grayson."

"Not for me there isn't."

He pulled up to the curb of my building and I climbed out.

"I'll see you later, Damon," I spoke as I shut the door and walked inside.

Stepping into my office, I turned on the light, set my briefcase down and took a seat behind my desk. Pulling my phone from my pocket, I sent Harper a text message.

"Good morning. When you get here come straight to my office."

"Good morning. I'll see you soon."

I sighed as I turned my chair around and stared out into the busy morning streets of the city as I sipped my coffee.

"Morning, boss," I heard Christine speak as she stepped inside.

"Morning." I turned my chair around.

"Here are the reports you wanted first thing. I'm surprised you beat me here this morning."

"I wanted to catch up on a few things. Thanks for the reports. Keep an eye out for Harper. I told her to come right to my office when she gets in."

"Will do. Do you need anything else?"

"No. I'm good."

I was looking over the reports when there was a light knock on my door.

"Come in."

The door slowly opened, and when I looked up, I saw Harper walk in with a smile on her face and her hand behind her back.

"Good morning. You wanted to see me?" She grinned.

"Good morning." I returned her smile as I got up from my seat and grabbed the Starbucks bag from my desk. "I got you something." I held out the bag to her.

The smile on her face widened.

"I got you something too." She held the exact same bag from Starbucks.

We took the bags from each other and opened them. Inside, was a cranberry muffin."

"I can't believe you bought me a cranberry muffin." Her face lit up like a kid on Christmas day.

"And I can't believe you did the same for me."

"I stopped at Starbucks on my way in and I saw it and had to buy it since you liked it when we shared one."

"I did the same thing." I smiled as I leaned in and kissed her soft lips. "Thank you."

"You're welcome. And thank you. Is that why you wanted me to come here right when I got in?" she asked.

"Yes. I wanted to surprise you and now we're both surprised. How is the design coming?"

"It's coming along. I have a couple things left to do, and then the first draft will be ready for you to see."

"Good. I can't wait to see it. How about we meet at one o'clock?"

"I'll put you in my calendar." She smirked.

"And I'll put you in mine." I winked.

She walked out of my office and just as I pulled the muffin out of the bag, my phone rang.

"Grayson Rhodes."

"Grayson, it's Conrad."

Shit.

"Conrad, how are you?"

"Listen, I hear you're having someone else design the high rise."

"You've heard correct."

"What gives, Grayson? You know we do all your building designs."

"I know. I hired a new employee and I'm having her take a shot at it. She had some designs in the back of her portfolio that caught my attention, so I figured why not."

"Does your grandfather know about this?"

"My grandfather is aware and doesn't have an issue with it. Listen, Conrad. This is my company and I decide who designs our buildings. If you're worried about losing our account, then you should be after this phone call. Nobody questions the decisions I make. Understand me?"

"I'll be talking to your grandfather about this."

"Go ahead and talk to him. We're done here."

I ended the call and threw my phone across my desk. I couldn't wait until this company was fully mine. Because as soon as it was, Conrad and his company were fired.

CHAPTER 22

Harper

I walked out of Grayson's office with the Starbucks bag in my hand and I could see the looks some of the women gave me and I could hear the whispers as I passed by. I ignored them and went into my office. Sitting down at my desk, I smiled as I opened the bag and took out the cranberry muffin Grayson bought for me. The way he made me feel was unlike anything I'd ever felt before. I'd never connected with anyone like I did with him, especially last night. Being with Grayson made me realize that the feelings I had for Kevin were nothing compared to what I felt for him. I wasn't falling in love with Grayson Rhodes, I already had fallen.

"Whatcha eating?" Curtis asked as he walked into my office.

"A cranberry muffin from Starbucks. Want some?"

"No thanks." He held up his hand. "I'm not a fan of cranberries. How is the high rise coming along?"

"See for yourself." I turned my computer screen around.

"Damn. You did all that?"

"Yes. Do you think Grayson will like it?"

"Hard to say. He's very particular."

"Listen, when I was walking to my office earlier, I noticed some of the women giving me looks and whispering. Have you heard anything?"

"I know a couple of the women aren't happy you're here. They think Grayson is playing favorites and they don't like it. But don't let them bother you. They're just jealous because you're a beautiful woman and well, they're them." He smirked.

"I need to finish this project before one o'clock. That's when I'm meeting with Grayson."

"Sure. If you need anything I'm right down the hall."

"Thanks, Curtis."

I headed down the hall to use the restroom. As I was in the stall, I heard the door open and two women walked in. I sat and listened as they carried on a conversation at the sink.

"I don't know why Grayson thinks she's so special. I don't even think she's that pretty."

"Right? I'm sure he's using her to his advantage like all the other women. It just pisses me off that I asked him if I could work from home a couple days a week because I didn't have a babysitter for my kid, and he said no. Then he hires that bitch and lets her do whatever the hell she pleases."

"Whatever is going on between them won't last. He'll get tired of her soon enough like he always does with women."

I waited until they left before leaving the stall. I would not let what they said get to me because they were nothing but insecure and jealous women.

It was one o'clock, so I grabbed the 3D printout from the printer and headed down to Grayson's office.

"Perfect timing." He grinned. "I just got off a conference call. Bring the printout over to the table." He gestured.

I did as he asked and spread it out. He looked it over as silence filled the room for what seemed like an eternity. I was nervous that he hated it. Shit. What if he did? What if I totally fucked this whole project up? The sick feeling that arose in my belly wasn't from the baby, it was nerves.

"I must say, this is unique with the scalloped edging. What made you do that?"

"Just like you said, it's unique. Pretty much all the high rises in this city look the same. I believe if you add a building that stood out amongst the rest, especially an apartment building, it'll gain attention which is what you want. You want to fill all 260 apartments before they even complete the building. This is a building people will talk about. It's unique, but classy. The wealthy people are always trying to outdo each other and want to be the talk of the town, and what better way to do that than to buy an apartment in a building that's so different from everything else and different from what everyone else lives in."

"You know what, Harper? I think you're on to something here. I like it."

"You do?"

"Yes." The corners of his mouth curved upwards. "The build will cost more than I originally expected, but that's okay. I'll send this out and have a model made. I knew I made the right decision by having you design this."

"Thank you, Grayson. Can I talk to you about something?"

"Of course. You can talk to me about anything."

"There's been some talk around the office about me and how some employees feel you're giving me special treatment by letting me only work in the office two days a week."

"Is there now?" he asked as he brought his hand up to my cheek. "Ignore them and the talk. It's none of their concern what I do. And if they want to hold it against you, then they'll be punished for behaving like children. That I can promise you. Okay?"

"Okay." I softly smiled.

"Good girl." His lips brushed against mine. "Why don't you take the rest of the day off? I'll have Curtis email you a couple projects for you to work on for the rest of the week."

"Are you sure?"

"Yes. I have a dinner meeting tomorrow night, so how about we get together Friday night? I'd like to see you again."

"Friday will work." I smiled as the fluttering in my belly began.

"We'll have dinner at my place, and if you're willing, I'd like you to spend the night with me."

"I'd love too."

"I was hoping you'd say that." His hand softly stroked my cheek. "I'll swing by and pick you up after work."

"I'll be ready."

CHAPTER 23

Harper

Laurel, Charlotte, and I climbed out of the cab, entered the medical building and took the elevator up to the third floor. After signing in, I took a seat next to my best friends as we waited for them to call my name.

"Thanks for coming with me."

"You know we wouldn't miss this for the world." Charlotte smiled.

"Yeah. We told you we'd be with you every step of the way," Laurel spoke.

"Harper." I heard my name called.

Getting up from our seats, I weighed in and then we were taken to room three where we waited for Dr. Graham to come in.

"You only gained three pounds. Is that normal?" Laurel asked. "Shouldn't you have like gained more?"

"I think three pounds is enough right now." I laughed.

"Good afternoon." Dr. Graham smiled as she stepped inside the room. "How are you feeling, Harper?"

"I'm feeling great, Dr. Graham. Except for being tired all the time."

"That's perfectly normal in your first trimester. As soon as you hit your second trimester that will subside. Lay down for me and pull up your shirt."

She grabbed the transducer and pulled the ultrasound machine closer to the table. After squeezing the warm gel on my belly, she placed the transducer on me, pressed down, and began moving it around.

"Here's your baby, Harper." She smiled.

Tears started to fill my eyes as I watched the screen and saw my baby for the first time.

"And here's the heartbeat. Nice and strong."

Charlotte and Laurel both gave my hands a squeeze as they watched the monitor.

"Ah, look at that little peanut," Charlotte spoke.

"Everything looks good, Harper. Your baby is growing right on schedule." Dr. Graham took a cloth, wiped the gel from my belly, and helped me up. "Here are a couple pictures for you and I'll see you in one month." She smiled. "If you have any difficulties or something doesn't seem right to you, call me."

"Thank you, Dr. Graham."

As we walked out of the medical building, I couldn't stop staring at the picture of my baby.

"That was so cool," Laurel said. "Who's in the mood for Thai?"

The restaurant was pretty crowded, but we were lucky enough to get a table by the window. After placing our order, I picked up my water, took a sip and prepared myself to tell them I'd slept with Grayson.

"So, Harper, how's Grayson doing?" Laurel asked.

"Funny you should ask. I slept with him two nights ago."

"What?!" Charlotte blurted out. "And you're just telling us now?"

"I know and I'm sorry. I wanted to wait until today to tell you in person."

"How was he?" Laurel asked. "We want every last detail."

"It was magical. I can't even put the experience into words. I'd never felt that way during sex before," I spoke as I chewed my bottom lip.

"Shit. So now what?"

"I don't know. I made dinner for him the other night and he brought me a dozen pink roses. Then the next morning, he bought me a cranberry muffin from Starbucks and gave it to me when I got into the office."

"Isn't that what you shared the first time you met?" Charlotte asked.

"Yeah." I smiled.

"That's so romantic. Sounds like someone is in love," Laurel spoke.

"I'm going to his place for dinner tomorrow night and he asked me to stay the night."

"Shit. Seriously? I need to meet this guy," Laurel said. "It's not fair that Charlotte already did. I feel left out." She pouted.

"You'll meet him soon. I promise." I let out a light laugh.

"Don't you think this is happening a little too fast?" Charlotte asked.

"Maybe it is but it just feels right. I think he's the one. The man I've been searching for my entire life."

"Whoa." Charlotte put her hand up. "You barely know this guy. The timing just seems weird to me. You decide to have a baby on your own and then suddenly, this guy appears in your life, gives you a job, moves you in to the building his company owns and doesn't give a shit that you're pregnant with someone else's baby. I don't know, Harper, something is bothering me about this whole situation. Grayson Rhodes is a millionaire, and he's number one on the New York's most eligible bachelor's list. Guys like him just don't settle down. Especially with a woman who's pregnant."

I was growing angrier by the moment listening to her spew her words.

"You sound like you're jealous, Charlotte."

"I'm not jealous, Harper. I'm being honest with you. This isn't like you. Especially after what happened with Kevin. The most important thing in your life is that baby you're carrying, and that's what you should be focusing on. Not a man like Grayson Rhodes."

"Charlotte, I think you should just stop," Laurel spoke.

"Why? Because I love her enough to express my feelings about this situation. I don't trust a man like him, and you shouldn't either." She pointed at me.

"What's this really about?" I asked. "Are you implying that I'm not good enough for someone like him? That I'm only destined to date assholes?" I voiced louder than I should have.

"That is not what I'm saying. I just don't want to see you get hurt again. You're trusting way too quickly, and I think you're not using your head when it comes to Grayson Rhodes."

"No!" I stood up from my chair. "You're just jealous because you can't find a decent man of your own. You're just a lonely hairstylist who keeps getting ghosted from every guy you meet up with. I'm not hungry anymore. I'm going home." I walked away.

"Harper, wait!" Laurel exclaimed, and I ignored her and left the restaurant.

I was furious with what Charlotte said. How dare she? She'd always been honest and opinionated but this time she took it too far. I went home, threw my purse down and started the water for a bath. I was hurt. So hurt by my best friend's actions.

The last time I'd heard from Grayson was last night when he texted me goodnight. I felt the need to reach out to him, so I sent him a text message.

"Can you talk for a minute?"

A moment after I sent that text message, my phone rang, and it was him.

"Hello."

"Hey. I only have a few minutes. I'm on my way to a meeting. Are you okay?"

When I heard the sound of his voice, the anger I'd felt went away.

"Yeah. I just wanted to talk for a minute."

"I can tell by the sound of your voice something is wrong. Talk to me, Harper."

"It's silly. I just had a fight with Charlotte, and I said some things I shouldn't have."

"What did you argue about?"

I couldn't very well tell him that the argument was about him and how Charlotte didn't trust him.

"It was really nothing. I'm sorry to have bothered you with this. I just wanted to hear your voice."

"Don't apologize. You'll work things out with Charlotte. She's your best friend and the two of you can't stay mad at each other for very long. Listen, I just got to my meeting, so I have to go. Are you going to be okay?"

"Yeah. I'll be fine. Thanks for calling."

"You're welcome. I'll call you later tonight."

"Okay."

I ended the call, climbed in the bathtub and then changed into my pajamas. It was only four o'clock, but I didn't care. I was tired and I just wanted to be comfortable. Plus, I wasn't going anywhere the rest of the night, and I had projects to work on that Curtis sent me.

CHAPTER 24

Grayson

I shook my head and placed my phone back in my pocket. Girl drama. I rolled my eyes. After I left the office, I met Julius at Edward's in Tribeca. He wasn't there yet, so I grabbed us a table and ordered us a couple beers.

"Sorry I'm late," he spoke. "Traffic is a bitch and the cab I was in almost got in a fucking accident."

"Traffic is always a bitch, my friend. You know that. We've lived here our whole lives. Besides, I've been telling you to get your own driver. I'm sure Yasmin would love you for that."

"She already loves me. Besides, I'm not extra like you." He smirked as he picked up his menu. "Thanks for the beer, bro. I really need it today."

"Bad day at the office, dear?" I smiled.

"Just a shit show. I had to fire one of my employees for incompetence. He mixed up someone's sperm samples and the woman who came in to get inseminated almost ended up with the wrong sperm. It's a good thing Cassie noticed it first. So, I'm afraid to ask. How are things going with Harper?"

"I slept with her," I spoke with an arch in my brow as the corners of my mouth curved upward.

"Why am I not surprised."

"She's mine now. She's all in and everything is going perfect according to plan. My grandfather wants to meet her as soon as he gets back from his trip. Once he does and I show him I'm in love with her, all that nonsense about signing the company over to Alfie will disappear."

"And you're not developing any feelings for her at all?"

"No. How could you even ask that? You know me, Julius, and you know where I stand with women and relationships. Harper already called me today all upset because she had a fight with one of her best friends and she wanted to talk." I sighed. "It's that kind of shit I can't stand."

"I hope you were nice to her about it."

"Of course, I was. I listened and offered her a piece of advice. I have to play the concerned boyfriend, don't I?"

"Oh. So now you're official?" His brow raised as he took a sip of his beer.

"Not yet. But we will be before my grandfather gets back. I'm having her over tomorrow night for dinner and I've asked her to spend the night. Of course she was more than happy to accept." I smirked.

"You, my friend, are a cold-hearted bastard. I'm not sure why I even associate myself with you."

I rolled my eyes as I picked up my beer.

"You seem to have forgotten that you were exactly like me at one time. The only difference is I'm not stupid enough to fall in love." I gave him a wink. "I was thinking that maybe the four of us can have dinner Saturday night at Per Se. Are you and Yasmin available?"

"Yasmin left for Chicago this morning and she's going to be gone for about a month. Her aunt is very ill and she's going to take care of her. I'm going to fly there and spend the weekends with her starting next weekend."

"Then it'll just be the three of us."

"Bro, I don't know. I know you said she won't recognize me, but what if she does?"

"She won't. And whatever you do, don't tell her you're the director at the cryobank."

"So you want me to lie to her as well?"

"You have no choice, or she'll get suspicious. She's a smart woman. You don't think she'll start running scenarios in her mind if she knew her baby came from your sperm bank? Do you think she'll think it's a coincidence?"

"Then what am I supposed to tell her I do if she asks?"

"I don't know. Tell her you're a financial guy or something."

"I hate every second of this and you know it." He pointed at me.

"You worry too much. We'll meet for dinner Saturday night and then you really won't have to see her much after that."

By the time I got home, it was nine o'clock. I told Harper that I'd call her tonight, so I poured myself a bourbon, sat down on the couch and dialed her number.

"Hello."

"Hey there, beautiful girl."

"Hi there, handsome. How was your dinner meeting?"

"It was good. How are you doing? Feeling any better than this afternoon?"

"Yeah. I guess. You're right. We'll work things out."

"Good. I'm happy to hear that."

"I don't think I told you, but I had a doctor's appointment this afternoon."

"Why? Is everything okay?"

"Yeah. It was my monthly appointment. I had an ultrasound done, and I heard the baby's heartbeat. I can't wait to show you the ultrasound picture tomorrow night."

I gulped and suddenly, I started to profusely sweat.

"That's great. I can't wait to see it. Did Curtis send you those projects?"

"He did and I'm working on one of them as we speak."

"Great. You can fill me in tomorrow. Listen, I just got home, and I have a few things to do. I'll see you tomorrow when I pick you up."

"Looking forward to it."

"Me too. Goodnight, Harper."

"Goodnight, Grayson."

A picture. She had a picture she couldn't wait to show me of her baby; my baby. Shit. That's the last thing I wanted to see. I sighed as I finished off my drink, went upstairs to change and then headed down to my study to check my emails.

CHAPTER 25

Harper

I awoke the next morning by my phone dinging with a text message from Laurel.

"I hope you're up. I'm on my way over for a bit before I have to go to work. See you soon. If you're not up, I'll be pounding on your door."

Rolling my eyes, I messaged her back.

"I'm up. I'll unlock the door. Just walk in."

After going to the bathroom, I was brushing my teeth when my phone dinged with a text message from Grayson. Instantly, a smile crossed my face.

"Good morning. I can't wait to see you tonight. Have a good day."

"Good morning. I can't wait to see you either. I'll have a good day only if you do."

"I'll have a perfect day knowing I'm going to see you later." He sent the winking emoji.

"Me too." I replied with the blushing smiley emoji.

I heard the door open, so I slipped on my robe and walked out of the bedroom.

"I bring gifts." Laurel grinned as she held up a carrier containing two coffees and a brown bag from my favorite breakfast place: The Broken Yolk.

"I hope there's a Jack's scramble bowl in that bag."

"Of course there is. I know it's your favorite."

I grabbed the coffee cup that had a "D" on it for decaf, grabbed two forks from the drawer, two napkins and took them over to the table.

"Thanks, Laurel. I appreciate it."

"You're welcome, sweetie. Yesterday was rough, and I wanted to give you some space. You know Charlotte means well. She's just worried about you, especially now with the baby coming."

"She need not worry about me. What is your feeling about everything?"

"I'm happy if you're happy. I do think things are moving rather quickly, but for some couples it happens."

"He sent me a text message this morning telling me he can't wait to see me tonight. Do you know how that makes me feel? After Kevin, I questioned everything about me. What I did or didn't do. What I could have done differently but didn't."

"Harper, Kevin was just a straight up asshole. There was nothing you did besides love him. He broke up with you out of his own insecurities. It had nothing to do with you."

"Maybe you're right."

"I am right. I know guys like him. I am the woman version of him." She laughed.

"True." I laughed with her.

"Just take a piece of advice, or not. It's up to you. Don't rush things with Grayson. I know he pays attention to you, buys you beautiful flowers and muffins, and all that's great, but don't forget who you are as a person. You're one of the strongest women I know, and you've been through so much since your parents died. Don't lose that strength and become dependent on a man who may or may not ultimately stick around for the long haul. Everything is rainbows and fairy dust right now. It always is in the beginning and you know it. As soon as the red flags pop up, take a step back and really think about things. Don't wait until all the flags are out and trying to wave some sense into you."

"I know." I sighed.

I'd spent the day working and getting ready for when Grayson came to pick me up. I packed a small overnight bag with a piece of sexy lingerie I wanted to wear before I couldn't fit in it anymore. I knew tonight would be perfect because any time I'd spent with him was.

"I'll be at your apartment in about ten minutes. Are you ready?"

"I am. See you soon."

I smiled as I threw my phone in my purse and set my bag on the table. Running into the bedroom, I took one last look at myself in the full-length mirror and gave my hair one last brush before I heard a knock at the door. He was right on time.

"Hi." I grinned as I saw him standing there looking as sexy as ever in his dark gray designer suit.

"Hi." He leaned in and kissed my lips.

"Come in. I just have to grab my purse and my bag."

"I'll grab your bag. Is that it over on the table?" he asked.

"Yes."

While he took my bag, I grabbed my purse and got out my keys to lock the door. My heart was racing as we took the elevator down to the lobby. I couldn't wait to spend the night with him.

"Have a good evening, you two." Sammy smiled as he tipped his hat.

"Thank you, Sammy. We will." Grayson smiled.

I turned around and gave Sammy a small smile and wave. He returned my gesture with a wink.

"Hello, Damon," I spoke as he held the door open for me.

"Hello, Harper. How are you this evening?"

"I'm great. How are you?"

"No complaints."

I climbed into the Escalade and Grayson slid in beside me, grabbing my hand and holding it.

"How was your day?" he asked.

"It was good. I got a lot of work done. How was yours?"

"Not bad, but certainly much better now." The corners of his mouth curved upward.

Damon pulled up in front of a tall brown building in Lenox Hill. Grayson opened the door, slid out first and then extended his hand and helped me down. The best part was he didn't let go while he held my bag in his other hand.

"Good evening, Mr. Grayson."

"Good evening, Charles. This is Miss Harper Holland. She's to be put on the list."

"Nice to meet you, Miss Holland. I'll add her now."

"What list?" I asked as we walked to the elevator.

"My guest list of people who are allowed to come right up to my penthouse."

"Why Mr. Rhodes, I'm feeling a little special right now." I grinned.

"Good, because you are special." He leaned in and kissed my lips as the elevator doors closed.

As soon as the doors opened, I was greeted by a magnificent foyer that consisted of white marble flooring and a beautiful oval curved staircase.

"Wow, Grayson. This is magnificent."

"Thanks. I'll give you a tour. We can start upstairs since I'm taking your bag up."

I slowly walked up the stairs, noting the gray painted walls and the dark cherry wood floors that greeted me. The hallway was long with guest bedrooms and bathrooms on each side, and all the way down at the end was the master bedroom that sat behind two large wood carved white double doors.

"Wow. Look at all these windows." I smiled. "This view must be breathtaking at night."

"It is. You'll be able to see it for yourself later."

I ran my hand along the gray down comforter that made up his bed. Across from it was a large fireplace and a massive TV that hung on the wall. A large cherry wood dresser graced the other wall with an armoire that sat in the opposite corner. The curtains that housed the tall floor to ceiling windows were the same gray as the comforter was. The room was decorated to perfection. Even the artwork that hung on the walls was of taste.

"Are you an interior decorator in your spare time?" I asked.

He let out a chuckle. "No. I hired an interior designer named Adalyn Grant. Her husband, Harrison, is a friend of mine. I bought this place in a foreclosure auction for practically nothing, but it desperately needed a remodel. So, I brought Adalyn in and she worked her magic."

"I haven't seen the rest of the house yet, but from what I can already tell she's fantastic at her job."

"She's actually the best. Come on, I'll show you the rest of the place." He held out his hand.

Taking it, he led me down the stairs and showed me the media room which housed two sectionals, a pool table and a large TV that took up most of the wall. When we entered the living room, the first thing my eyes noticed was the grand piano in the corner. It just wasn't any old piano.

"Is this a Steinway Grand?" I asked as I walked over to it and ran my hand over the satin ebony finish.

"It is." He smiled.

"These cost like fifty thousand dollars."

"Yes. They do."

"Do you play?" I asked as I wouldn't take my eyes off it.

"I do play. You must know something about pianos yourself if you recognized it was a Steinway right away."

"My mother started teaching me the piano when I was about four years old. Actually, I don't think I was even four yet. Her grandmother was a concert pianist who traveled the world. She taught her how to play. She told me her dream was to buy a Steinway Grand and one day she'd have one where we both could sit and play. After she died, and they sent me to live with my aunt, I was lucky enough that she had a piano for me to play. But I could only play it when she wasn't home. If I even dared to try to play it when she was sleeping or hungover, she'd scream at me for an hour."

"Did she play?"

"No. The house came with the piano and she liked to use it for a place to throw her clothes. She never wanted to learn to play. Who taught you?" I asked.

"My grandmother. She started teaching me when I was young just like your mother taught you. What cooking is to you is what the piano is to me."

"Wow. I can't believe it."

"Sit down and play something for me."

"Oh, my God. No, Grayson, I can't."

"Yes, you can." He placed his hands on my hips and made me sit down on the black tufted bench. "This is your chance to play on a Steinway Grand. Are you really going to turn it down?"

"I guess not." I bit down on my bottom lip as I looked up at him.

I stretched out my fingers and took in a deep breath as I softly stroked a couple keys to get a feel for it and to listen to the magnificent sound it made. I started to play Bohemian Rhapsody by Queen. Before I knew it; I was lost in the music. I played as if I only played yesterday. Grayson stood there with his arm on the edge of the piano smiling as I unleashed my talent. I finished the song, and he slowly clapped his hands.

"Are you sure you're not a professional in disguise?" He smiled. "I'm pretty sure you inherited your grandmother's talent. That was phenomenal, Harper."

"Thank you. God, it felt so good to play again. It's been a long time. Your turn. I want to hear you play." I smiled.

"I'll play something for you later. Dinner should arrive any minute."

CHAPTER 26

Grayson

When she said she could play, I had no idea she could play that way. Shit. Something we both had in common. Charles called up to let me know that dinner had arrived. The elevator dinged and two people dressed in black attire stepped out with large warming bags in their hands.

"Good evening, Mr. Rhodes. Would you like us to set up in the dining room?"

"Yes. It's this way."

I led them into the dining room. Harper took her seat, and I grabbed her a glass of water and myself a bourbon.

"What did you do?" Her face lit up with a smile.

"Not much." I winked.

One server removed two large plates from his bag which consisted of filet and lobster tail, parmesan red potatoes and steamed green beans. The other server set the large salad in the middle of the table and a platter of fresh hot bread with honey butter.

"I'll put the dessert in the refrigerator," he spoke.

"Very good. Thank you."

THE DONOR

I reached into my pocket, pulled out some cash and handed each of them a generous tip.

"Thank you, Mr. Rhodes. Enjoy your dinner."

"We will. Thank you."

I took my seat across from her and picked up my fork.

"This looks delicious, Grayson. Thank you."

"You're welcome. I hope you like filet and lobster. After I ordered it, I started to have doubts and thought maybe I should have asked you first."

"I love filet and lobster. You did good."

"Just so you know, I had a backup plan if you didn't like it."

We talked over dinner about work. When we finished, she got up and started cleaning the table.

"Go sit down. You're my guest and I'll clean up."

"You were my guest and still insisted on helping, so I'm doing the same thing. Plus, it'll be quicker if we both do it. I'm eager to hear you play the piano." She grinned.

"There's dessert in the refrigerator," I spoke.

She placed her hand on her belly. "I will definitely have dessert later. I'm so full. Dinner was delicious. Thank you." She reached up and brushed her lips against mine.

"You're welcome. I'm happy you enjoyed it."

"Oh. I'll be right back. I want to show you something," she spoke with excitement.

"Okay. I'll be in the kitchen."

A moment later she returned.

"This is my baby." She grinned from ear to ear as she held the ultrasound picture in front of me.

My heart started to rapidly beat, and a wave of heat took over me as I stared it.

"See. There's the head and that right there is a little arm."

I gulped and didn't know what to say.

"Wow. I've never seen an ultrasound picture before. Do you know the sex?"

"I won't know that until my next ultrasound in a few weeks."

"Are you going to find out?" I casually asked.

"Yes. I want to know so I can decorate the nursery and start buying the color appropriate clothes. You know, blue for a boy and pink for a girl."

"Sure. I don't blame you."

Looking at the picture was making me uncomfortable, and I needed to change the subject before she noticed.

"When are you due?"

"November 16th."

I inhaled a sharp breath as the heat in my body consumed me.

"Are you okay?" she asked.

"Yeah. It's just November 16th is my birthday."

"Oh my God! You're kidding. Wow. Talk about crazy."

"It sure is." I turned away and placed the plate in the dishwasher. "I can finish cleaning the rest up later. I want to play the piano for you."

Truth was, I needed to sit and play for my own sanity. My baby was due on my birthday. What the fuck. I took her hand and led her over to the piano where we both sat down on the bench and I began to play Fur Elise, but a darker more intense version. When I was finished, I looked over at her and the smile she had on her face.

"That was hauntingly beautiful, Grayson. Fur Elise, right?"

"Yes. I tweaked it a little bit."

"You're really good." She kissed my cheek. "May I?" She placed her hands on the keys.

"Of course, take it away."

"I would ask you to join me but I'm not sure you'll be able to keep up." Her smile widened as her fingers began to move across the keys and she played Boogie Woogie.

I grinned as I sat there for a moment and let her play solo before joining in. Placing my fingers on the keys at the end, I joined in and we played together. I added in a few extra notes and she didn't even flinch. She kept playing right in tune with me. We swayed back and forth as we laughed until we played the final note.

"I can't believe you!" She laughed.

"I can't believe you!"

I placed my hand on her cheek and stared into her beautiful blue eyes.

"You're truly a terrific woman, Harper," I spoke with seriousness.

"And you're truly a terrific man, Grayson."

I leaned in and kissed her soft lips. Then I stood up, picked her up from the bench and carried her up the stairs to my bedroom. I couldn't forget how her skin trembled under my fingers and how good it felt to be buried deep inside her.

After stripping out of our clothes, I brought her on top of me and watched her beautiful body move back and forth as she rode my cock. I cupped her perky breasts in my hands and softly stroked her hardened peaks with my thumbs as her moans grew louder and she came. It took every ounce of strength I had in me to hold back. She rolled off me and laid on her belly as she tried to catch her breath. I thrust inside of her, both of us gasping at the same time. My cock was still rock hard and ready to explode as I thrust in and out of her. One final thrust and I released myself inside her, moaning at the intense pleasure.

I collapsed on top of her as I tried to regain my breath, grabbing her hands and interlacing our fingers as we lay there together for a few moments. Once both our heartrates calmed and our breathing returned to normal, I rolled off her and held out my arm as she snuggled her body against mine and laid her head on my chest.

"So, what kind of dessert did you get?" she casually asked.

I let out a chuckle. "Cheesecake with fresh berries. Would you like a piece?"

"I'd love some. I seemed to have worked up quite an appetite."

"Me too." I kissed the top of her head. "I'll be right back. Don't move."

I climbed out of bed, pulled on my pajama bottoms and went down to the kitchen. After cutting two pieces of cheesecake and putting it on one large plate for us to share, I grabbed two forks from the drawer and went back upstairs. I stopped in the doorway and stared at her with a smile on my face as she lay there sound asleep.

CHAPTER 27

Harper

My eyes flew open as the sun peered through the slits of the blinds that covered the windows. I couldn't believe I fell asleep last night and didn't wake up once. I rolled over and stared at Grayson while he slept. The last thing I remembered was him going downstairs to get us some cheesecake. Shit. Now I was totally embarrassed that I fell asleep before he got back. What a way to end a perfect evening. He stirred before opening his eyes.

"Good morning." A soft smile graced his face. "Were you watching me sleep?"

"Maybe." The corners of my mouth curved upward.

"That's okay because I was watching you sleep last night." His finger ran down my cheek.

"I am so sorry about that. I don't even remember closing my eyes."

He rolled on his back and stretched out his arm. That was my queue to snuggle against him.

"Don't apologize. You were tired and I understand that. Did you sleep well?"

"I did," I spoke as my head lay on his chest and I softly stroked it with my fingers. "Your bed is very comfortable."

"Good. I'm happy you like it because if I have my way, you're going to be spending a lot of time in it."

"Is that so?" I smiled as I lifted my head and stared at him.

"It is so." He gave me a wink. "I wanted to ask you something last night before you fell asleep. My best friend, Julius, asked us to have dinner with him tonight. His wife is out of town and he wants to meet you. Plus, I want you to meet him too."

"I'd like that."

"Good. I'll call him in a while."

"Do you by any chance have decaf coffee?" I asked.

"No. I don't. But hold on a second."

He reached for his phone on the nightstand and called down to the lobby.

"This is Grayson Rhodes and I need someone to run out and get me some decaf coffee for my Keurig. Make sure it's a dark roast. And if you could hurry it up, it would be greatly appreciated. Thank you."

"I can't believe you just did that. I could have run out and got some. You didn't need to send the staff to do it."

"Trust me. They don't mind. Especially when they know they're getting a large tip."

"I'm starving. Would you mind if I whipped us up something for breakfast?" I asked.

"Not at all. I don't have much though. My maid usually goes to the grocery store on Mondays."

"You have a maid?"

"Yes. She comes twice a week to clean and prep meals for me. Do you think I can clean this big place myself?"

"Would you even clean it yourself?" I smirked at him.

"No." He chuckled. "Come up here."

I scooted myself up, so my lips were mere inches from his. He softly pressed them against mine. Suddenly, his phone rang.

"Thank you. Bring it up," he spoke.

"Your coffee has arrived, madame." His smile brightened my morning.

While I climbed out of bed and slipped into my pajama bottoms and tank top, Grayson grabbed some cash from his wallet and headed downstairs. I followed and went into the kitchen to see what I could whip up. First thing I did was pop a k-cup in his Keurig and made him a cup of coffee.

"Here you go." He kissed my forehead.

"And here you go." I handed him his coffee.

"Thank you. I'm going to quickly take a shower and give Julius a call. Did you find anything to make?"

"I did." I beamed.

"Okay. I'll be back in a flash. Thanks for the coffee." He held his mug up.

After I made myself a cup, I grabbed the eggs from the refrigerator along with some tomatoes, spinach, onion and a green and red pepper and some cheddar cheese. Today's breakfast would be a veggie omelet and toast.

"Perfect timing," I said as I plated his omelet and buttered toast.

"This looks delicious. Thank you." He leaned in and brushed his lips against mine.

We took our plates and sat on the stools at the island.

"I called Julius and we'll meet him at Eleven Madison Park at six o'clock."

"Okay. Sounds good. I can't wait to meet him."

"I hope you don't mind but I made plans for us for today. You have nothing going on, do you? Again, I probably should have asked you first."

"The only thing I have going on is spending the day with you." A smile crossed my lips.

"I was hoping you'd say that. There's a new butterfly exhibition over at the Museum of Natural History I've been wanting to see."

"I heard about that. I like butterflies."

"Good. Then we'll go there first and play the rest of the day by ear. Sound like a plan?"

"Sounds like I plan." I smiled.

After I finished my breakfast, I took a quick shower, applied some light makeup, and grabbed my jeans from my bag. As I pulled them on, I struggled to button them, but it wasn't happening. Shit!

"What's wrong?" Grayson asked as he saw me lying on the bed in my unbuttoned jeans.

"We have to stop at my place on the way to the museum."

"Why?"

"Because my jeans don't fit anymore. I can't button them."

He started to laugh, and I threw a pillow at him.

"I'm sorry but what did you expect? You're pregnant. Eventually your clothes aren't going to fit you anymore," he spoke as he held out his hand and helped me up.

"I know but I didn't think it would happen yet." I pouted.

"Jeans are tight to begin with. Put on the pants you were wearing yesterday, and we'll go to your place so you can change into a different pair. You'll be okay." He kissed my forehead.

We left his penthouse and stopped by my apartment on the way to the museum. I changed into a pair of black leggings, a tank top and a long cardigan. Spring had sprung in New York, and the need for a jacket was no longer needed. At least during the day.

We entered the museum and looked around before it was our time to enter the Butterfly Conservatory. I watched Grayson as he looked at the butterflies that flew around us with the corners of his mouth slightly curved upward.

"My mother loved butterflies," he spoke. "We had a vacation home in Montauk that we'd spend our summers at and in the back yard she had a huge garden with at least twenty different butterfly houses. She'd spend most of the afternoon out there watching them and taking photographs. She said they were the most beautiful creatures on Earth. My father used to call her the butterfly whisperer, because when she'd go out in the garden, butterflies would land all over her. They made her happy."

"That's a beautiful memory." I took hold of his hand.

"Yeah. I guess it is. Since we're in this beautiful place surrounded by butterflies and plants, I need to talk to you about something."

"Sure. What do you want to talk about?"

"I would like it if we were exclusive."

"Grayson Rhodes, are you asking me to be your girlfriend?" I grinned.

"I suppose I am. And when you meet my grandfather, I'd like to introduce you to him as just that."

"Yes." I threw my arms around his neck. I'd love to be your girlfriend."

"Phew. I was worried for a minute. I know this is moving a little fast."

"Just a little. But when you know, you know. Right?" I kissed his lips.

CHAPTER 28

Grayson

I hated that word "girlfriend." It was enough to make my skin crawl. But I had no choice. It had to be done. There were too many expectations from women who had the title. They wanted gifts, cute little love notes or text messages all the damn time. When you had a bad day and just want to be alone, they wanted answers as to why and when you didn't give them, they accuse you of shutting them out. They want apologies first even though they were in the wrong because they are always right about everything. If you dare glance at another woman or even speak to her, they're convinced your cheating on them. They think we're mind readers and when we fail at doing something, they thought we should have done, they become psychotic. They think they should be number one priority and nothing else in the world should matter. Been there. Done that. Hence, the reason I stay as far away from relationships as possible. Now that Harper thinks we're in a committed relationship, I can stop trying so hard. But I had to be careful and keep things working as smoothly as possible between us until I got my company.

We left the museum and because it was a nice day outside; she asked if we could go to Central Park for a while.

"Is there any specific area of Central Park you want to go to?" I asked her.

"Bethesda Terrace."

We walked hand in hand through the entrance of the park and headed to Bethesda Terrace.

"Is there a specific reason you wanted to come here?" I asked as we approached it.

"This is the reason I moved to New York," she spoke.

"You moved to New York because of this place?"

"Yes. My parents loved New York City and once a year, we'd vacation here for a week. This is where my father asked my mother to marry him. Right on these steps. He got down on one knee, told her how much he loved her and then asked for her hand in marriage. We'd come visit here every year. My mother's face would always light up when she told me the story. After they passed away, I knew the only place I could ever be close to them again was here. Whenever I need to think or I miss them, I come here for a while. That's why I attended NYU and never left New York after I graduated."

"I'm sorry, Harper." I wrapped my arms around her and kissed the side of her head.

"It's my special place and I want to share it with my child and tell him or her all about their grandparents."

I didn't know what to say, so I just held her for a moment.

It was six o'clock on the dot when we walked through the doors of Eleven Madison Park. Julius hadn't arrived yet, so I told the hostess to bring him to our table when he arrived.

"Hey, bro." He smiled.

I got up from my chair and gave him a light hug.

"Julius, I'd like you to meet Harper Holland. Harper, this is my best friend, Julius."

"It's a pleasure to finally meet you, Harper." He smiled as he extended his hand.

"It's great to meet you, Julius."

He took his seat. While we both ordered bourbons, Harper ordered water and a decaf coffee.

"So, what is it you do?" she asked him.

I could sense the nervousness inside him.

"I'm a stockbroker for a capital management company on Wall Street."

"Wow. That must be an exciting job." She smiled.

"Oh. It has its perks. So, Grayson tells me you're pregnant, and you used a sperm donor."

I kicked him under the table. I couldn't believe he said that.

"Yes. I am, and yes, I did." Her lips formed a small smile.

"Well, I think the decision you made was a great one. I truly admire a woman who knows what she wants and goes after it." He grinned.

"Thank you, Julius. I appreciate that."

※

She laid in my arms as her head rested on my chest. We'd just had sex and we were both tired.

"Thank you for today. I had a great time," she softly spoke.

"You're welcome. About tomorrow, I have some things I need to take care of, so I'll take you home after breakfast. Think about where you would like to go."

She lifted her head from my chest and looked at me with a wide grin across her face.

"How about Alice's Tea Cup? Their Wonderland Waffles are the best."

"I can honestly say I've never eaten there. But if that's where you want to go, then we'll go." I tapped her nose.

The next morning after we got dressed, we went to Alice's Tea Cup. The line to get in was long and there was over an hour wait.

"This is a bit ridiculous," I said.

"Maybe we should have made reservations last night. Oh well. We can go somewhere else." A look of disappointment filled her face.

"You really want those waffles?"

"I do but we're not waiting an hour. We can make reservations and come back another time."

"No. Hold on." I held up my finger.

Walking up to the hostess desk, I pulled a hundred-dollar bill from my wallet and folded it up.

"Excuse me. Are you sure the wait is an hour?" I discreetly slipped the young brunette the bill.

She looked at it and then up at me.

"Let me check. I'll be right back."

After a moment, she returned with a smile on her face.

"The table you reserved is ready. Follow me."

I called over to Harper, who was standing by the door.

"I got us a table." I winked at her as we followed the hostess.

"How?"

"I slipped her some cash in exchange for a table. You want waffles from here and you will have them."

"You're so sweet, Grayson. Thank you. Also, my baby thanks you." She smiled.

I swallowed hard as I picked up the menu and looked it over.

"It's very whimsical in here," I said as I looked around.

There were families all around us. Parents with small children. Some were behaved and others not so much. It was noisy. A little too noisy for my taste. I'd be fine if I never had to come back here again, even though I did enjoy the smoked salmon benedict. I'd kept waiting for Harper to ask me what my plans were for today, but she never did.

After breakfast, I took her back to her apartment. Setting her bag down on the floor, I wrapped my arms around her.

"Enjoy the rest of your day. I'll see you tomorrow morning at the office."

"Thanks. You too."

I brushed my lips against hers and kissed her goodbye.

CHAPTER 29

Harper

As soon as the door shut, a part of me felt a sadness, but the other part of me was on cloud nine. Grayson Rhodes was now my boyfriend, and I was his girlfriend. A smile crossed my face every time I thought about it. I needed to apologize to Charlotte for the things I said, and I knew if I called her, she wouldn't answer. Sundays were cleaning day, so I knew she'd be home.

I hailed a cab to her apartment and rang the buzzer.

"Who's there?"

"Char, it's me. We need to talk."

"Why? So you can continue to tell me how jealous I am of you."

"Please. I miss you."

She buzzed me in, and I walked up the stairs to her apartment. When I reached it, she stood there with her arms folded staring at me.

"I'm sorry." I pouted. "It's the pregnancy hormones."

A small smile formed on her lips and she held out her arms for a hug.

"I'm sorry too. Come on in. I'll make us some tea and we'll talk."

I took a seat on the couch while she made our tea.

"I miss you, Charlotte."

"I miss you, Harper."

She walked over, handed me my tea and then took a seat on the couch next to me.

"There's something I need to tell you," I said as I carefully sipped from the cup.

"What is it?"

"Grayson asked me to be his girlfriend. We're officially a couple now."

She reached over and placed her hand on mine.

"Does he make you one hundred percent happy?" she asked.

"Yes, he does. I'm in love with him."

"Then that's all that matters to me. You know I've always been protective of you since the first day we met. You've had so much heartache and now you're finally having what you always wanted. I just want you to be incredibly happy."

"I know you do, and I am. Not only does having this baby make me happy, but so does Grayson. I really want you to give him a chance."

She reached over and hugged me.

"I will give him a chance, but if he hurts you," she broke our embrace, "I'll cut off his balls with my scissors."

I let out a laugh.

Suddenly, the buzzer rang.

"That's probably Laurel. She said she might stop by this afternoon," Charlotte spoke.

She buzzed her in and when Laurel opened the door and saw me sitting on the couch; her face lit up.

"Please tell me the two of you made up," she said.

"We made up." Charlotte smiled."

"Thank God. The two of you were exhausting me."

I told Laurel about me and Grayson and she got all giddy with excitement.

"I want to meet him, Harper."

"You will. I promise. We just have to figure out a good time."

"So where is he today?" Charlotte asked.

"He had things to do. I'll see him tomorrow morning at the office." I smiled.

※

Grayson

I picked up Julius, and we attended the Rangers game. When we entered the suite, there was a spread of food waiting for us on the table.

"Good afternoon, gentlemen." The bartender in our suite spoke. "May I get you anything?"

"Good afternoon, Danny. Two bourbons."

We filled our plates with food, grabbed our bourbons and took our seats overlooking the arena.

"I like Harper," Julius said. "She seems like a great woman and I hate what you're doing to her."

"Yes. You've already expressed your honesty at least a million times already. We are officially a couple now." I choked out the words.

"What? You asked her to be your girlfriend?"

"I did. I asked her yesterday, and she graciously accepted. She'll be meeting my grandfather soon and he needs to see that I'm serious about her."

"And when are you going to tell him she's pregnant?"

"I'll tell him after he meets her."

"Did you tell her we were coming to the game today?"

"No. I tested her. I told her I had things to do, and I patiently waited for her to ask me what I was doing, and she didn't. She just said okay and not another word about it. To be honest, it impressed me."

He rolled his eyes at me as he finished his drink.

"She can't button her jeans anymore. I had to take her home yesterday before we went to the museum so she could get another pair of pants. Soon she'll start showing and that gorgeous little body of hers will no longer exist."

"Duh. That's what happens when women are pregnant."

"I know that, but I like her body the way it is now. There's something that's bothering me."

"What? What on Earth could possibly bother you?" he asked in a smug tone.

"What if I can't get hard the further along she gets? I'm not attracted to pregnant women. How do I explain that?"

"You don't, and then your little plan will come to an end. Have you forgotten who you're talking to here? Whose family business revolves around helping women get pregnant."

"She showed me her ultrasound picture the other night."

"And? What did you say?"

"Not much. I said it was cool and then I quickly changed the subject."

"How did you feel when you saw the picture of YOUR baby?"

"I felt nothing," I spoke as I stared straight ahead at the game.

CHAPTER 30

ONE WEEK LATER

Harper

I took in a deep breath as Grayson opened the door to his grandfather's home.

"Don't be nervous. He's going to love you." He smiled as he gently squeezed my hand.

An older woman walked into the foyer with a wide grin on her face.

"Grayson. It's good to see you." She pinched his cheek.

"Celia, I'd like you to meet my girlfriend, Harper Holland. Harper, this is my grandfather's housekeeper, Celia."

"It's such a pleasure to meet you. You're beautiful." She gave me a light hug.

"Thank you. It's nice to meet you too."

"Grayson, I thought I heard voices in here."

"Grandfather, I'd like you to meet my girlfriend, Harper Holland. Harper, this is Leon Rhodes, my grandfather."

"It's nice to meet you, Mr. Rhodes." I smiled.

"The pleasure is all mine, Harper. Come." He took hold of my hand and led us into the living room. "Dinner will be ready shortly. Sit down. Can I offer you a glass of wine?"

"No. I'm good thank you."

Grayson walked over to the bar and poured himself a drink.

"I saw the design you did on the high rise. I must say, Harper, I was impressed."

"Thank you, Mr. Rhodes."

Dinner was served and Grayson grabbed hold of my hand and led me into the dining room. The dinner Celia made was excellent as well as the fruit flan for dessert. We had a great conversation and I really liked Grayson's grandfather.

"It was such a pleasure to meet you, Harper," he spoke as he lightly kissed my hand. "I'll be making sure I stop by your office when you're there."

"Thank you, Mr. Rhodes. I had a lovely time." I smiled.

"Are you ready, sweetheart?" Grayson asked as he took hold of my hand.

That was the first time he'd called me that and it made my heart flutter.

One Week Later

Grayson

It had been a week since my grandfather met Harper and I needed to tell him she was pregnant before he noticed on his own. Just as I pulled my phone out to call him, there was a knock on my office door, and he stepped inside.

"Grandfather, I was just going to call you?" I held up my phone.

"Were you now?" He smiled. "Well, I'm here. I just came in to check up on some things."

"I wanted to know if you'd have dinner with me tonight at Daniel."

"Sure. Is Harper joining us?"

"No. I thought it could just be the two of us."

"Okay. I stopped by her office to say hi and Curtis said she wasn't in today."

"She doesn't work in the office on Thursday."

"All right. I have some things to do. What time do you want to meet for dinner?"

"Seven o'clock?"

"I'll see you then."

※

I arrived at Daniel promptly at seven o'clock and my grandfather was already sitting at a table waiting for me with a drink in his hand.

"How long have you been here?" I asked as I sat down.

"About five minutes."

The waiter walked over and took my drink order as we looked at the menu.

"So what prompted this dinner?" my grandfather asked. "I will assume it has something to do with Harper."

"Actually, it does. You didn't give me your thoughts about her."

"I like her, Grayson. I like her a lot. She has a good head on her shoulders, she's smart and very nice, not to mention she's beautiful. You did good, son."

"Thank you, Grandfather. I'm happy you approve of her. But there's something I haven't told you yet."

"What?"

"She's pregnant."

"Is the baby yours?"

"No. Before I met her, she was already pregnant. The father isn't in the picture at all."

"I see. And you knew this when you met her?"

"Not at first. She told me during the interview and when I offered her the job."

"And yet you still pursued her?"

"I did. How could I not?" I smiled.

"You really love this girl, don't you?"

"I do. For the first time in my life, I finally understand what love is."

Damn. I was good.

"I can tell she feels the same way about you. I was watching her at dinner and every time you spoke her eyes lit up. I'm proud of you, Grayson. I knew one day you'd meet someone who would steal your heart. I just can't help but wonder about the timing though. It wasn't too long after I gave you that ultimatum you met her."

Shit.

"She isn't some random girl I just picked up. I told you how we met. She was in front of me in line at Starbucks and we got to talking about the cranberry muffins. The more we talked, I found out she was looking for a job and I had her come in for an interview. I had no intentions of pursuing anything with her at that point. But the more time I spent with her and got to know her, the more my desire to be with her grew."

"Like I said. You did good, and I'm proud of you for wanting to take on the responsibility of her pregnancy."

I gave him a smile as I finished my drink.

CHAPTER 31

FOUR WEEKS LATER

Harper

The past couple of months had been the happiest months of my life. Between being pregnant and having Grayson by my side, my life was perfect. I was now sixteen weeks pregnant and in my second trimester. The tiredness I'd felt in my first trimester was gone and I had a lot more energy. Not to mention I was always horny as hell.

"I need to go shopping this Saturday for some new clothes. Would you like to come with me?" I asked Grayson as I softly stroked his arm while he worked on his laptop.

"Why don't you ask Charlotte and Laurel. I'm sure they'd love to go with you."

"Oh. Okay. I thought we were going to spend the weekend together," I said.

"We will. We'll see each other when you come back from shopping and then we have the whole day Sunday. We can do whatever you want." He glanced over at me.

"Sure. I'll text them right now and ask. And don't forget I have my ultrasound on Monday morning. I told you about it a couple weeks ago."

"Shit."

"What?"

"I'm sorry, sweetheart. I can't go with you on Monday."

"Why not?"

"Because I have that big meeting with the contractors for the high rise."

"I thought it was tomorrow."

"It originally was, but I had to reschedule because my grandfather wants to be there, and he isn't coming back until Sunday. I'm sorry. I totally forgot."

"It's okay. I understand," I spoke with disappointment. "I'm going downstairs to grab a bottle of water. Do you want anything?"

"I can get it for you." His lips pressed against the side of my head.

"I'll go. You stay here and work."

I climbed out of bed and went down to the kitchen. I wouldn't lie and say that I was fine with him not going with me to the ultrasound. I wasn't. I was hurt and disappointed. He knew how important this ultrasound was and I'd be finding out the sex of the baby. Of course, I wanted my best friends there, but I wanted the man I loved to share in the joy with me. I grabbed a bottle of water from the refrigerator and took it over to the piano. Placing my hands on the keys I began to softly play Brahms Lullaby. It wasn't too long before Grayson came down and leaned against the piano.

"What are you doing?"

"Playing for the baby," I spoke without even looking at him. "I'll be up in a minute."

"Okay." He kissed the top of my head and went upstairs.

He still hadn't said those three little words every woman longed to hear from the man she loved: I love you. I'd been waiting for him to say it first. Doubt crept in my mind about how he truly felt for me. He didn't want to go shopping; he couldn't go to my ultrasound, and he never told me he loved me. Shit. Maybe I was just overreacting and being a hormonal pregnant woman. I stopped playing, went upstairs and climbed into his bed.

"Are you okay?" he asked.

"Yeah." I smiled. "I'm just tired."

"Let's go to sleep." He smiled as he ran the back of his hand down my cheek.

Leaning over, I gave him a passionate kiss and then laid my head on his chest as his arm wrapped tightly around me.

"I love you, Grayson."

"Me too, sweetheart." He kissed the top of my head. "Goodnight."

It felt like my heart had stopped. What the fuck was that? He couldn't even say the words to me. Tears sprung to my eyes as I slowly closed them.

The next morning, I climbed out of bed before his alarm went off, grabbed my clothes, and went home. I wanted to be alone and away from him for a while. It wasn't too long after that I received a text message from him.

"I'm assuming you went home since I couldn't find you anywhere in the house. What's going on?"

"I wasn't feeling well, and I didn't want to wake you."

"What's wrong? How aren't you feeling well?"

"I just feel a little nauseous and I have a really bad headache. I hope I'm not coming down with the flu or something."

"You could have stayed here in bed all day. You didn't have to leave."

"I just wanted my own bed."

"Do you need me to bring you anything before I head to the office?"

"No. I'm good. I'm going to lay down. Have a good day at work."

"Okay. I want you to rest all day today. I'll check in with you later."

I stayed in my pajamas all day just because I felt like it. I didn't want to go out and I didn't want to do anything but binge watch Gilmore Girls on Netflix. It was around one p.m. when my phone rang, and Grayson was calling.

"Hello?"

"Hey. How are you feeling?"

"Not too good." I lied. "Still battling this nausea and headache."

"Do you think you should call the doctor?"

"No. This is the same thing Charlotte had last week. I'm sure I got it from her. I'll be fine. I'm just lying on the couch watching TV."

"I'll come over after I leave the office and bring you some soup."

"That's sweet of you, Grayson, but I don't want you to catch this bug."

"I was already exposed, Harper."

"Actually, when I'm sick I just like to be alone. I'm weird like that."

"Oh. Okay. Promise me you'll call me if you need anything."

"I will. I love you," I softly spoke in anticipation of his response.

"Me too. Talk to you later."

CHAPTER 32

Grayson

I met Julius for lunch at the Gray Goose in Soho. I didn't like the way Harper just left this morning without even telling me she was leaving. I didn't like her being alone when she wasn't feeling well, and her not wanting me to come over tonight bothered me.

"I think something is going on with Harper," I spoke to Julius as I picked up my drink.

"What do you mean?"

"I think she's pissed at me."

Julius let out a chuckle. "Why? What did you do?"

"Nothing. I did nothing. Everything was fine up until last night when we were lying in bed and she asked me to go clothes shopping with her on Saturday. I told her to ask Charlotte and Laurel because I thought that would be a great girl's day out. Then she reminded me of her ultrasound appointment on Monday, which I told her I can't go."

"And why can't you go?" His brow raised.

"For one, I don't want to go, and second, I have a contractor's meeting for the high rise."

"A meeting you purposely scheduled so you had an excuse as to why you couldn't go with her." He pursed his lips.

"Perhaps." I sipped my drink. "She told me last night for the first time that she loved me."

"Oh boy. I was waiting for that. And you said?"

"Me too. When I got up this morning she was gone. She said she wasn't feeling well and wanted to go home. I just spoke to her right before I got here and offered to bring her some soup tonight and she said she likes to be left alone when she's sick."

"Uh-oh. You're in trouble, bro." He pointed at me. "If you're going to continue with your plan, you better hurry up and make things right."

"What are you talking about?"

"She's pissed off at you. Not only did you turn her down when she asked you to go shopping, you can't go to the ultrasound, and you didn't tell her you loved her back. When women start thinking about shit, watch out."

"I told her. I said, 'Me too'. What's wrong with that?"

He sighed as he rolled his eyes at me.

"Are you kidding me? 'me too' doesn't mean shit. It's not the same thing. It's like you're agreeing with her that you love yourself."

"See." I pointed at him. "This is the shit I don't need in my life."

"Well, you're stuck now until you get your company. I would advise you to take control of the situation ASAP. It's supposed to be a gorgeous day on Sunday. Surprise her with a picnic lunch in Central Park. Get those little finger sandwiches, a couple of different salads, some different cheeses and crackers and dessert. I'd say a bottle of wine, but she can't drink, so water will do. But make it the sparkling kind."

"You're kidding me, right?"

"No. I'm not. Trust me. I've done it with Yasmin. Works like a charm. You pull off a romantic afternoon picnic, all will be forgiven and forgotten."

I sighed as I finished my drink and asked the waitress for another one.

When I returned to the office, I asked Christine to step inside.

"Have a seat." I gestured. "I need you to do me a huge favor."

"Of course. What do you need?" she asked.

"I need you to go to the store. I don't care where you go, but I need a large picnic basket and a blanket."

"Okay. May I ask why?"

"I'm taking Harper on a picnic Sunday. Also, where can I get little finger sandwiches and picnic type of food?"

"There's this cute little French bakery in Greenwich village that does stuff like that. I can go there today and place an order. I think they deliver."

"You're a lifesaver, Christine. Thank you. I'll have Damon pick you up and take you."

A couple of hours later, Christine walked into my office.

"The basket and blanket are with Damon. I got them both at Pottery Barn. As for the lunch, I placed an order with the bakery, and they will deliver it to your home on Sunday at eleven a.m."

"Excellent. Thank you, Christine. I appreciate it."

"You're welcome." She smiled.

I looked at my watch and it was six o'clock. Picking up my phone from my desk, I gave Harper a call with the hopes she'd changed her mind about me coming over.

"Hello."

"Hi, sweetheart. How are you feeling? Any better?"

"A little bit."

"Enough for me to bring you some dinner?"

"I already ate, and I'm exhausted so I'm going to bed early."

"Alright. I'll miss you tonight."

"Me too. Talk to you soon."

She ended the call before I could even say goodbye. What the fuck? I didn't need this shit. Julius had plans tonight with his parents, so I called a couple other friends of mine and met them at Randolph's bar and lounge at the Warwick Hotel. As we were sitting on the barstools drinking and talking, this beautiful woman with long fiery red hair sat down next to me.

"Hi, handsome. How about buying me a drink?" The corners of her mouth curved upward.

"I'd love too." I smiled.

We talked for a while and I could tell she wanted to fuck me.

"Listen, I'm leaving New York tomorrow to fly back home. I have a room upstairs if you'd like to come up and have a nightcap." She flirtatiously smiled.

"Let's go."

I said goodbye to my friends, placed my hand on the small of her back and took the elevator up to her room. The moment we stepped inside, we kissed. My hands roamed up and down her body, and as she reached for the button on my pants, I grabbed her hands and stopped her.

"I'm sorry. I can't do this," I said.

"Why? Are you married?"

"No. I'm not. I just can't." I walked out of her room and headed home.

The only thing I saw in my mind when I kissed that woman was Harper. Shit. Why the fuck did I feel so guilty?

CHAPTER 33

Harper

I awoke the next morning to a text message from Grayson that he'd sent at midnight.

"I'm sure you're sleeping so I just wanted to say goodnight and I hope you're feeling better. I'll talk to you tomorrow. Sweet dreams, sweetheart."

I was still mad and hurt so I didn't bother messaging him back. I got up, showered and put on some makeup before Laurel came over. Charlotte would meet up with us after she was done with her client.

"Let's stop at Starbucks for a coffee before we shop," she said. "What's wrong? I can tell you're off."

I sighed as we walked into Starbucks and stood in line.

"It's Grayson."

"What's going on? Are you two fighting?"

"Tell me if I'm being hormonal or if I have a right to be upset."

We ordered our coffee and waited to the side for them to be made.

"I asked him to go with me today, and he suggested I call you and Charlotte. Then I reminded him about the ultrasound appointment on Monday, which I told him about two weeks ago and he said he'd go. But now, he forgot and scheduled this big contractor meeting."

"Wow. Really? I'm sorry, Harper."

They called out names for our coffee, so we grabbed them, walked out and headed down the street.

"If you want my honest opinion, I don't think you're being hormonal. You're a woman in love and you want your boyfriend at the ultrasound with you. It's perfectly natural to be angry with him now that he can't go even though he said he would. It's an important time, you know?"

"There's something else. I told him the other night that I loved him for the first time."

"Wow. What did he say?" She smiled.

"He said 'me too.'"

"What?" Her face twisted. He didn't say I love you back."

"No. So I got up the next morning and went home before he woke up. I told him I wasn't feeling well, and I didn't see him at all yesterday. He wanted to come and bring me dinner after work, and I told him no. I'm really mad at him, Laurel, and I don't want to see him right now."

She hooked her arm around me. "I don't blame you one bit. But you will have to eventually talk to him."

"I know." I sighed.

"Cheer up, buttercup. We have some serious shopping to do." She grinned.

As I was in the fitting room trying on some clothes, my phone rang, and Grayson was calling.

"Hello."

"Where are you? I'm at your building and Sammy said you and Laurel left. I thought you were sick."

"I'm feeling a little better today and I told you I needed to go shopping. Remember? You told me to ask them because you didn't want to go."

"Sweetheart, it's not that I didn't want to go. I just thought it would be fun for you girls to do it together. And you didn't take my card I left on the dresser for you the other night."

"I don't need it. I can buy my own clothes. Thank you."

"Why didn't you text me back this morning?"

"I woke up late and had to hurry and get ready. I was going to text you later."

"Speaking of later, how about doing something tonight?"

"I don't think that's a good idea. I'm already getting tired and I'll probably just sleep when I get home."

"Oh. Okay. Well, I have plans for us tomorrow, so I'll be coming by to pick you up at noon."

"What plans?"

"It's a surprise. One I think you'll like very much."

"Okay. I have to finish trying on these clothes. I'll talk to you later."

I ended the call before he could say another word. Hopefully, I'd be over my anger with him by tomorrow. But I wasn't so sure. Charlotte met up with us and I explained everything that was going on to her. I could see the look in her eyes of disapproval. She still never fully trusted Grayson.

After we finished shopping, I headed home and Sammy helped me with my bags.

"Wow. It looks like you went on quite a shopping spree."

"I needed all new clothes, Sammy. This baby is growing every day." I placed my hand on my belly.

"I can see that. Mr. Rhodes stopped by earlier and was looking for you."

"I know." I rolled my eyes. "We're having a little spat right now. Or actually, I'm a little irritated with him."

"I'm sorry to hear that. If you ever want to talk, you know where to find me."

"Thank you, Sammy. You just might be sorry you said that." I smirked.

"Somehow, I doubt that, Harper. Enjoy the rest of your day."

I hadn't heard from Grayson except earlier in the afternoon when he called me. I sat on the couch, turned on the Gilmore Girls, and wondered what he was doing. Hell, I didn't care. Okay, maybe I did, but I wasn't about to text him and ask. He said he'd pick me up tomorrow, so I'd just wait to talk to him then. What surprise could he have planned for me?

Grayson

I had Julius over for a guy's night since Harper still didn't want to see me. We ordered a couple pizzas, drank, and played a few games of pool.

"I'm taking Harper on a picnic tomorrow in Central Park."

"Good boy." He grinned. "She's still mad?"

"I think so. I wanted to do something with her tonight, and she turned me down. See, this is the reason why I don't get into relationships. All of this is such bullshit."

"But your relationship isn't real. So why do you care if she's mad at you?"

"Because. What if she breaks up with me and then I don't get my company?"

"She isn't going to break up with you. She loves you. She's just upset. She'll get over it after the picnic tomorrow. Then you can go on pretending to care about her and upsetting the balance of her life once you get the company and dump her." His eye narrowed at me.

"Thanks, bro. I appreciate your honesty." I glared at him.

"Just remember, she's the mother of your child."

"Knock it off, Julius." I hit the eight ball in the left corner pocket.

After Julius left, I checked my phone to see if Harper had texted me. She didn't. What the fuck. I sighed as I poured myself another drink and took it out to the terrace where I stared out into the brightly lit city. Damn it. I needed to make sure she was okay, so I sent her a text message even though it was late, and I was sure she was sleeping.

"Hi sweetheart. I was just checking in to see how you're doing?"

I stared at my phone and impatiently waited for the three dots to appear. Nothing.

"You must be asleep. I can't wait to see you tomorrow. I miss you."

Hopefully seeing those messages when she wakes up will put her in a better mood.

CHAPTER 34

Harper

The moment I woke up, I grabbed my phone and read Grayson's messages. He was making an effort, so I decided to text him back.

"Good morning. I miss you too. See you at noon."

I had just finished curling my hair when there was a knock on the door. Opening it, Grayson stood there holding a bouquet of a dozen red roses in his hand.

"Hi." He smiled.

"Hi."

"These are for you."

"Thank you. You shouldn't have."

"I wanted to."

I took the roses from him and wrapped my arms around his neck as he held me tight.

"I hope you're feeling better," he spoke as he broke our embrace and kissed me.

"I am." I smiled.

"You look absolutely beautiful. Is that a new dress?"

"It is." I did a little twirl. "I bought it yesterday."

"Well, it looks great on you. Are you ready to go?"

"Let me just slip on my shoes."

We walked down to the lobby and Sammy gave me a wink and smile as Grayson and I walked out the door hand in hand.

"Good afternoon, Harper." Damon smiled as he held the door open.

"Good afternoon, Damon. Thank you."

I stepped inside and Grayson slid next to me.

"Where are we going?"

"You'll see when we get there." He grinned.

Damon pulled up to the entrance to Central Park. Climbing out, with the help of Grayson, it was the same entrance to get to Belvedere Castle. Damon unlocked the trunk and handed Grayson a blanket and picnic basket.

"A picnic?" I brightly smiled.

"Yes. We're having a picnic in Central Park," he spoke as he hooked his arm around me.

We set up in a quiet little spot on the lawn next to Belvedere Castle. The view was amazing, and I was quickly forgiving him. He opened the picnic basket, took out two plates, two bottles of water, some finger sandwiches, a quinoa salad, cut up fruits and veggies, cheese cubes and crackers.

"I can't believe you did all this."

"Why? Do you think I'm not capable of being romantic?" He smirked.

"No." I laughed. "This is just awesome." I threw my arms around him. "Thank you."

"You're welcome, sweetheart. So, tell me about your day with the girls yesterday."

While we ate, we talked. We talked about my day, his day, music, certain poetry, etc. Everything but the reason why I was hurt and upset. I just needed to put it in the past and move on.

It was a beautiful sunny day with a light wind that swept across us every now and again. Grayson stretched out his legs, and I laid on my back with my head resting on his lap. It was a perfect picture. Apparently, someone else thought so because a nice older couple who appeared to be in their seventies stopped and asked if I would like them to take a picture of us like that.

"What a beautiful young couple. Oh, I see you're expecting. First child?" the older woman asked.

"Yes." I smiled.

"Would you like me to take a picture of you two? This is something to always be remembered."

"Thank you so much. That would be great." I reached for my phone and handed it to her.

"You two just sit there like you are and look at each other. Isn't this so romantic, Henry? It reminds me of us of when we were their age. Here you go," she spoke as she handed me my phone. "Enjoy the rest of your lives together and congratulations on your baby."

"Thank you," both me and Grayson spoke as they walked away hand in hand.

I looked at the pictures she took of us and I nearly lost my breath. She snapped two pictures, and they were perfect.

"Would you like me to send these to your phone?" I asked Grayson.

"Of course, I would."

We lay there for a while, soaking up the sun and enjoying the beautiful warm weather. When it was time to leave, we packed up and headed to my place.

I gasped as his mouth explored my sensitive area and his hands groped my breasts. His skills always amazed me, and my body reacted as the earth-shattering orgasms took me over the edge. Hovering over me, he smiled as he brushed his lips against mine while he thrust inside me. My nails dug into the flesh of his back as he moved in and out at a steady pace. His teeth tugged at my hardened peaks as he softly licked them to soothe the sting. Moans erupted from us as we both were on the brink of an orgasm.

"Come with me, sweetheart. Please, come with me."

I let out a howl as my body shook and my legs tightened around him at the same time he exploded deep inside me. Tilting my head back, I gasped for air as I could still feel his hard cock resting inside me. There was no place I wanted to be but here with him, exactly like we were.

He kissed my lips and rolled off me while placing his hand over his heart.

"Are you okay?" I laughed.

"Yeah. I'm okay," he spoke with a smile as he tried to regain his breath.

We spent the rest of the evening eating Chinese food and watching a movie before heading to bed.

The next morning, Grayson climbed out of bed, showered, and put on one of the suits he'd left in my closet. He had some clothes here for when he spent the night and I had some clothes at his place which I needed to replace with some of my new clothes. While he was getting dressed, I went into the kitchen and made him a cup of coffee and toasted a bagel. Even though it was my scheduled day to go into the office, I decided to go tomorrow instead since today was my ultrasound appointment.

"Is that bagel for me?" He grinned as he walked in the kitchen, placed his hands on my hips and kissed me.

"Yes."

"Thank you."

He sat down at the table and checked his phone while he ate his bagel and drank his coffee.

"Aren't you going to eat?" he asked.

"I'm going to breakfast with the girls after my ultrasound." I turned away and went back into the kitchen.

As I was standing at the sink washing a glass, I felt his hands grip my hips from behind and the warmth of his breath swept across my neck.

"I'm sorry I can't go. You know I would if I could, right?"

"Yeah. I understand. You have an important meeting."

"Okay. I have to go." He turned me around. "We're going out to dinner tonight to celebrate your ultrasound. I'll have Damon pick you up before he picks me up at the office."

"Sounds good." My lips formed a small smile. "I love you."

He stared into my eyes for a moment before pressing his lips against mine.

"Me too. Good luck today and call me." He walked away and out of my apartment.

I sighed as I leaned against the sink. He still couldn't say those three words to me, and it hurt.

"Are you ready to see your baby and see how much he or she has grown since your last ultrasound?" Dr. Graham smiled.

"Yes. We're all ready." I grinned.

As happy as I was to be here, I wanted Grayson with me. A part of me didn't understand why he couldn't push the meeting back an hour so he could be here.

"Here's your baby, Harper. We have a nice strong heartbeat."

Tears sprung to my eyes as I stared at my growing baby on the screen.

"Oh my God!" Laurel exclaimed.

"That is so cool," Charlotte said.

"Everything looks perfect. The baby's measurements are right on point. Do you want to know the sex? I have a perfect view." She smiled.

"Yes, Dr. Graham. I'm dying to know."

"Congratulations, Harper. You're having a girl."

Both Laurel and Charlotte screamed in excitement as tears streamed down my face.

"I'll see you in a month." Dr. Graham smiled while she helped me up and then left the room.

"OH MY GOD! We're having a girl!" Laurel exclaimed while Charlotte was looking up at the ceiling thanking God.

I couldn't help but laugh.

"Think of all the shopping we can do now for her. Pink. Pink. Pink. Everything will be pink with bows and ribbons and lace. Cute little dresses and sunhats and shoes to match," Laurel said.

The three of us walked out of the office and headed around the corner to get some breakfast. As excited as I was, a part of me wanted to call Grayson and tell him. But the other part of me wanted to keep it from him as a punishment for not being there with me.

"Aren't you going to call Grayson and tell him?" Charlotte asked.

"No. I'll tell him tonight at dinner," I said as I looked over the menu.

"I thought you weren't mad at him anymore," Laurel spoke.

"I thought I wasn't either. I guess I'm not mad. I'm hurt."

"Sweetie," Charlotte grabbed my hand, "I get that you want to punish him, but he'll be there for everything else."

"I told him again today that I loved him, and he came back with the same response as always."

"Maybe he's scared to say it. You know, some men don't feel like they can live up to what the words mean," Laurel said. "Maybe that's his problem. It could be he's scared."

"Don't take this the wrong way, Harper. You know I love you," Charlotte spoke. "What does it even matter? I mean, look at Kevin. He told you all the time he loved you and then told you three months before your wedding he wasn't sure if he loved you enough to marry you. As far as I'm concerned, people toss those words around like it's nothing. So what if he doesn't say it back. Are you really ready to believe him anyway?"

"Charlotte." Laurel smacked her arm.

"It's okay, Laurel. She has a point. I'm just not going to say it anymore."

CHAPTER 35

Harper

It was six o'clock when I went down to the lobby and climbed into the back of the Escalade.

"How was your day, Harper?"

"It was good, Damon. I'm having a girl." I smiled.

"That's wonderful. Congratulations."

"Thanks. I haven't told Grayson yet, so act surprised."

"I will."

I hadn't heard from Grayson all day which kind of pissed me off. I figured he'd at least call to see how it went. We pulled up to the building and Grayson slid in next to me and gave me a kiss.

"I thought I told you to call me today," he said.

"Sorry. I was busy with Charlotte and Laurel. Plus I wanted to tell you in person."

"Okay. So tell me how the ultrasound went."

"It's a girl." I pulled the picture out and handed it to him.

"Wow. A girl." He smiled. "That's great, sweetheart." He leaned over and kissed me.

Grayson

I swallowed hard as I stared at the picture of my baby. I suddenly became heated and I noticed Damon staring at me through the rearview mirror as we were stopped in traffic. I loosened my tie.

"Is the air on?" I asked him.

"Yes. It's on."

"Well, turn it up or something. It's boiling in here."

I handed the picture back to her and she told me to keep it. Was she testing me?

"I have three of them. So that one is yours."

"Thanks," I said as I folded it and put it in my coat pocket.

I didn't know what else to say.

"Dr. Graham said the baby is growing well and right on point."

"Good. Good to hear. So, the baby is healthy?"

"Yeah. She's perfect." She smiled.

After we ate and left the restaurant, we went back to the penthouse. I really just wanted to be alone tonight. But if I suggested it, I would piss Harper off, and I didn't need to rock the boat any more than it was already rocking. As soon as she was asleep, I went downstairs, poured myself a drink and sat down at the piano, pushing one key at a time as I downed my bourbon.

The next morning, I got up before my alarm was set to go off and went for a run. I needed to clear my head. When I got back, Harper was already up and sitting at the island eating pancakes.

"I got the note you left. How was your run?" she asked.

"It was good."

"Are you hungry? I can make you some pancakes?"

"No. I'm just going to get in the shower. We need to leave soon for the office."

"Are you sure? The batter is already made?"

"I said I don't want any goddamn pancakes!" I shouted at her. "I'm going to take a shower." I walked away as I shook my head.

Harper

What the hell was that about? He'd never yelled at me like that before. I shook my head as I cleaned up the mess in the kitchen, slipped on my shoes, grabbed my purse and left his penthouse. As I was in the cab on my way to the office, a text message came through from him.

"Where the hell are you? I get out of the shower and you're gone."
"I have a lot of work to do so I left to get to the office early."
"Whatever, Harper."

Grayson

I threw my phone on the bed and changed into my suit. Maybe I shouldn't have yelled at her like I did, but I was on edge right now and I just wanted to be left alone. I grabbed my briefcase and headed down to the lobby where Damon was waiting for me.

"Where's Harper?" he asked.

"She went in early," I spoke with an attitude.

"Did the two of you have a fight?"

"No. We didn't have a fight. She's just acting like a child."

"Speaking of a child, I saw your reaction when you looked at that ultrasound picture. Are you having second thoughts about your plan?"

"No, I'm not, and I don't want to talk about it."

I walked into the building and took the elevator up to my office. It pissed me off that Harper left this morning, and I wasn't about to go see her just yet. Just as I sat down behind my desk, my grandfather walked in.

"Good morning, Grayson."

"Grandfather, good morning. You didn't say anything about coming in today."

"I have a meeting in an hour, and I need you to be there. I'll be in conference room one."

"Sure. What's the meeting about?"

"You'll find out in an hour." He smiled as he walked out.

I felt restless so I walked over to Harper's office to apologize.

"Hey." I lightly tapped on the door jam.

"Hey," she softly spoke.

I walked inside her office and shut the door.

"Listen, Harper. I'm sorry I yelled at you."

"What was that all about, Grayson?" she asked as she got up from her chair and walked over to me. "Are you having second thoughts about us because of the baby?"

"No, sweetheart." I wrapped my arms around her and pulled her into me. "Not at all. Things have just been crazy here at work and instead of talking to you about it, I just snapped. I'm sorry."

"You know you can talk to me about anything, right?"

"I know, sweetheart, and I promise from now on I will."

"Okay." She smiled as she kissed my lips. "You are forgiven."

"I need to get some work done. My grandfather called me into a meeting in about an hour."

"What's the meeting about?"

"I don't know. He said I'll find out when I get there."

"Good luck." She patted my chest.

&.

I walked down to the conference room and when I opened the door and stepped inside, I saw my grandfather and our lawyer, Bill Steinman, sitting at the table.

"Bill." I extended my hand. "What are you doing here? Don't tell me we're in some kind of legal trouble."

"Sit down, Grayson," my grandfather spoke. "There's something I need to tell you."

"What is it?" I asked with nervousness.

"Well, I decided to retire early and move to Florida. I've met a special woman down there and it's where I need to be. And now that you have Harper, it's time."

"What?" I asked in shock.

"It's going to take at least three months to get everything together for the transfer of ownership which Bill will be handling. In a matter of three months, the company will be yours, son. Of course I'll still be on the board, but you will have full control."

"Congratulations, Grayson," Bill said.

"Grandfather, I can't believe this."

"Believe it because it's happening. You're the backbone of this company and I know you're more than capable of running it yourself. You've proven yourself to me both personally and professionally. I'm proud of you."

"Thank you. Wow. Who is this woman?" I smiled.

"She's a special lady. You'll meet her. Don't worry."

"Another thing. I'm selling the townhome and was hoping you could hire Celia as your housekeeper. I know Harper doesn't live with you yet, but I'm sure it's coming and with the baby, you two could use the help."

"Yes. Of course."

"Thank you, son."

"Grayson, it was good to see you again," Bill spoke as he extended his hand. "The next time we meet you'll be signing the papers to your new company."

"Thank you, Bill."

CHAPTER 36

Grayson

I couldn't believe this was happening already. I'd never been happier in my entire life and I couldn't wait to tell Julius. Pulling out my phone, I dialed him.

"What's up, bro?"

"I have big news. Can you meet for lunch?"

"Sure. Where do you want to meet?"

"How about Ocean Prime at noon?"

"Sounds good. I'll see you then."

When I walked back to my office, I told Christine to have Harper come down.

"How did your meeting go?" she asked as she walked in.

I walked over, shut the door and placed my hands on her hips.

"The meeting went great. My grandfather has decided he's retiring early. Three months to be exact. Do you know what that means?"

"You're getting the company in three months?"

"YES!" I grinned as I picked her up, swung her around and kissed her lips.

"Congratulations. That's wonderful news! I'm so happy for you. We need to celebrate."

"Yes. We will definitely be celebrating tonight. I couldn't wait to tell you." I kissed her again.

I headed over to Ocean Prime and when I got there, Julius was already waiting for me.

"It's about time you got here," he said.

I glanced at my watch. "I'm five minutes late."

"Exactly."

I took off my suit coat and sat down across from.

"Thanks for already ordering my drink."

"You're welcome. You said you had exciting news. Spit it out. What's going on?"

"My grandfather has decided to retire in three months."

"What? Are you serious?"

"As serious as I've ever been."

"And?"

"He's transferring the company to me."

"YES!" he held up his hand for a high five. "Congrats, bro. That's excellent news. Look at that, in three months you can get rid of Harper."

I looked away as I picked up my glass.

"She's having a girl."

"Nice. You know what they say about daddy's little girls."

I threw the liquid down the back of my throat.

"You're off the hook in three months. You have to be happy about that, bro."

"Yeah. I am." I signaled the waiter for another drink.

---

*H*arper and I celebrated my big news by having dinner at Per Se and then going back to my penthouse and making love. She snuggled against me as my arm held her tight.

"I can't believe my grandfather is retiring so soon."

"He found true love again. He wants to spend all his time with her. They aren't getting any younger."

"I guess. It'll be weird not going to his home anymore. I know he travels a lot, but he always comes back."

"Oh my God, Grayson!" Harper exclaimed as she placed her hand on her belly.

"What?"

"I think I just felt the baby kick." She quickly sat up.

"Are you sure?"

"She just did it again." She smiled as she grabbed my hand and placed it on the side of her belly.

Suddenly, I felt a little flutter against my hand.

"Did you feel that?"

"Yes. I felt it!" I smiled. "Let's see if she'll do it again."

I watched her as she slept in my arms. She looked so peaceful, and I enjoyed having her in my bed. Quietly getting up, I reached in the pocket of my suit coat I wore yesterday and pulled out the ultrasound picture. I took it downstairs with me while I poured myself a drink. Taking a seat on the couch, I sat there and stared at it.

CHAPTER 37

ONE MONTH LATER

Grayson

I began to question everything I'd done. I was in love with her and I always knew it but couldn't admit it. I couldn't sleep. I was restless, and she knew something was wrong. I blamed work, but the truth was I needed to come clean about everything and tell her that the baby she was carrying was mine.

I leaned against the doorway of the bathroom and stared at her as she was in the bathtub. Her hair was twisted up and her belly stuck out above the water. She looked so damn beautiful especially when she looked at me with her baby blue eyes.

"Hey you." She smiled. "What are you doing?"

"Just admiring how beautiful you are." I smiled.

"Can you admire me while you soap up my back?" a grin crossed her lips.

I rolled up my sleeves and knelt down next to the tub. She handed me the loofah, and I poured some body wash on it and began slowly washing her back.

"Thank you." She smiled with a slight turn of her head.

"You're welcome."

"Can you help me out? If I stay in here any longer, I'll turn into a prune."

I took hold of her hand and helped her out. Grabbing a towel, I wrapped it around her and pulled her into an embrace.

"I love you, Harper," I whispered in her ear for the first time.

She broke our embrace and stared at me. I think she was in shock.

"I love you too, Grayson," she said as she placed her hand on my cheek.

I called Julius and asked him to come over for a guy's night since Harper was out with her friends. I needed to talk to him about my plan.

"No Harper tonight?" he asked as I took the burgers off the grill.

"She's out with her girlfriends."

"Just think, in less than two months, I won't be asking that anymore."

"That's what I want to talk to you about. I love her, Julius, and I can't let her go."

"What? Since when?"

"Since I first met her, I guess. I was trying to make myself believe that I wasn't. These past few months with her have been the best months of my life. I told her the other night that I loved her."

"Shit, Grayson. So now what? Are you going to tell her the truth?"

"I have to."

"Fuck! You can't. Do you know what she'll do to you? Do you understand that you will lose her and your kid forever? Not to mention if my family found out, I could lose my job."

"She'll be pissed. I know. But she'll appreciate my honesty. She knows I truly love her."

"It doesn't matter, bro. SHIT!" He paced around the room.

"We lied to her about my job. You don't think she'll retaliate by reporting me?"

"She won't. I'll tell her you wanted nothing to do with it and I made you. I need to be with her, Julius, and I want to raise our child together."

He pointed his shaking finger at me. "Have you forgotten that you signed away your parental rights? So even if she sues us both, you'll lose! Goddamn it, Grayson. I knew I never should have gone along with this."

"You did, and it's too late. I just need to work up the courage to tell her."

"Listen to me." He grasped my shoulders. "You don't need to tell her anything. Just keep on living your life with her. You know it's your kid. So tell her you want to adopt her and give her your name. She'll never have to know."

"And how are you going to explain your job? What about Yasmin? What if she tells her?"

"She won't. I'll make sure of that. Shit. We have to come up with something."

"No more lies, Julius. I can't do this anymore. I can't live the rest of my life with this secret."

"YES YOU CAN! You're fucking Grayson Rhodes. Your whole life revolves around secrets. Trust me. If you tell her, that'll be the end of your relationship FOREVER!"

CHAPTER 38

ONE MONTH LATER

Grayson

I tried to tell Harper everything, but something always held me back. I'd start the conversation with "I need to talk to you about something." And when she'd look at me with those beautiful eyes and a smile that was always on her face, I couldn't. The last thing I wanted to do was hurt her and cause her unnecessary stress for her and the baby.

We had just finished making love, and she was lying on her back against me while my arm held her. I reached over and placed my hand on her naked belly and held it there. She was now twenty-four weeks pregnant and growing every day. This was my future. A future I never saw coming for someone like me. She changed me and my life. She taught me about love and how truly special loving someone was. She gave me a purpose, and she made me a better man. A man I never would have become if it wasn't for her.

"I need to talk to you about something," I spoke.

"Okay." She smiled as she rolled on her side and looked at me.

I took in a deep breath.

"Are you alright?" she asked as she brought her hand up to my cheek.

I couldn't do it.

"You know how much I love you, right?"

"Yes. I know." A grin crossed her face.

"I would like you to move in here with me."

"What? Are you sure?"

"Yes. We can choose one of the guest rooms for the nursery and we'll decorate it that is fit for a princess."

"Grayson, I can't believe this. Yes. I'll move in with you. What about the lease on my apartment?"

"It's my building. I'll tear it up." I smirked.

She leaned in and brushed her lips against mine.

"I love you so much."

"I love you too, sweetheart."

Two Weeks Later

Harper

"I need to start packing soon," I said.

"I'm surprised Grayson didn't hire a service to do that for you." Laurel smirked.

"Trust me. He suggested it but I told him no. I'm capable of packing my own things."

"What are you going to do with your furniture?" Charlotte asked.

"Give it away to anyone who wants it." I smiled.

"Yes! I want your dining set and your living room set." Charlotte grinned.

"I wouldn't mind your bedroom set," Laurel spoke. "I could put it in the spare bedroom."

"It's yours."

We were in the middle of eating lunch at a cute little diner that had just opened up across from the cryobank when I looked up and saw Julius walk in.

"Hey. There's Grayson's best friend, Julius. I'm going to go say hi."

He handed the cashier his card, signed the receipt, grabbed his carryout bag and headed out the door before I could make it up there. I walked outside to see if I could catch him when I noticed him across the street and walking into the cryobank building.

"That's odd," I said to myself. "I wonder why he's going there."

My curiosity was peaked so I crossed the street, entered the building and saw him standing and waiting for the elevator.

"Mr. Chambers," a woman spoke. "Your one o'clock cancelled."

"Okay. Thanks for letting me know, Carla," he said as the doors opened, and he stepped inside.

When he turned to push the button to whatever floor he was going to, he saw me standing there. His eyes widened as the doors shut. This didn't make any sense. I walked up to the woman named Carla.

"Excuse me. That man who just got on the elevator. Does he work here?"

"You mean Mr. Chambers? Yes, he's the director. Why?"

Shit. I needed to come up with something quick.

"I purchased sperm from your bank." I placed my hands on my belly. "And I swear I went to high school with him."

"He's been the director for about seven years. His family owns the company."

"Oh. Then that wasn't him. My mistake. Thank you."

I turned and hurried out of the building. My heart was racing, and my body was shaking. Why would Grayson and Julius lie about where he worked? I walked back into the diner and sat down.

"Where were you?" Charlotte asked.

"I tried to catch up with Julius, but he was already gone."

"What's wrong?" Laurel asked. "You're as pale as a ghost."

"I'm not feeling well all of a sudden. I'm going to head home and lay down."

"Do you want us to come with you?" Charlotte asked.

"No. I'll be fine. I haven't been sleeping well at night because she's kicking a lot and I'm uncomfortable."

I went into my purse and pulled some cash out with my shaking hand.

"Lunch is on us," Laurel spoke.

"Thanks. I'll call you later."

I ran out of the diner, hailed a cab and took it back to my apartment. What the fuck was going on? I paced back and forth trying to figure it out. Grayson's best friend was the director of the New York Cryobank. The same bank I used to find a donor. And yet, both Julius and Grayson lied to me about where Julius worked. I paced around while recalling specific events in my mind. I went back to when I told Grayson about the baby and how I used a donor from the New York Cryobank. He could have told me then Julius worked there but he didn't. Shit. I needed my laptop which I left at Grayson's penthouse.

I ran out of the building and hailed a cab. When the driver pulled up to the curb, I threw some cash at him and ran inside the building.

"Good afternoon, Harper. Is everything okay?"

"Yeah. I left my laptop upstairs and I'm late for a Skype meeting."

I took the elevator up and saw my laptop sitting on the island. Running to it, I opened it up and pulled up all my emails from the cryobank, specifically the one with the profile for Donor 137665. I placed my hand over my mouth as I stared at it.

Donor 137665 is a highly educated, top of his class graduate from Yale. With his high I.Q. and competitive nature, he is extremely successful in the corporate business world. He has an outgoing personality and loves to socialize and meet new people. As an avid classical music lover, he relaxes by sitting down and playing music by Beethoven and Bach on his grand piano.

Height – 6'2
Weight – 190lbs.
Eye Color – Blue
Hair Color – Brown
Hair texture – Straight
Ethnic Origin – Caucasian
Ancestry – English, Irish, Scottish
Religion – None

Education Level – Masters
Areas of Study – Business, Finance, Investment Management
Blood Type – O+
Pregnancies – No
Expanded Genetic Testing – Yes
Instruments – Piano
Favorite Food – Mexican, Italian
Outdoor fun – Skiing and walks on the beach.

No. I shook my head. This can't be. Tears sprung to my eyes as I stared at the picture of Grayson when he was a child. I ran to his study and started going through his things. I sat down at his desk and opened the drawer on the right-hand side. The ringing of my phone startled me. It was Grayson. I let it go to voicemail while I opened the drawer on the left side and sitting there was a picture of him and his parents when he was a child. Grabbing it, I ran to my laptop and tears streamed down my face as I stared at both pictures of the same child. Instantly, I felt sick to my stomach, and I fell onto the stool. Grayson kept calling, and I kept letting it go to voicemail. My heart was racing out of my chest and I needed to calm down for the baby's sake. I slowly closed my eyes and took in three long deep breaths.

CHAPTER 39

Grayson

I was sitting at my desk when my phone rang, and it was Julius.

"Hey, Julius. What's up?"

"Grayson, she's going to figure it out if she hasn't already," he spoke in a panicked tone.

"Who? What are you talking about?"

"Harper. She just saw me at the cryobank."

"What?!" I stood up. "Did you talk to her?"

"No. I had just stepped in the elevator and I went to push the button and there she was, standing there. The doors shut before either one of us could say anything. Grayson, my name is at the top of the directory right where she was standing."

"FUCK!" I have to go."

I immediately dialed her, and it rang and then went to voicemail. So I kept trying as I ran out of the building. Goddamn it! Where was she? I called her apartment building and talked to Sammy.

"Sammy, it's Grayson Rhodes. Have you by any chance seen Harper?"

"Yes, Mr. Rhodes. She was here a while ago and then left. She was in quite a hurry."

"How long ago?"

"About a half hour."

"Thank you."

I ended the call and dialed my building.

"Charlie, It's Grayson Rhodes. Have you seen Harper by any chance?"

"Yes. Mr. Rhodes. She's upstairs now."

"Whatever you do. Do not let her leave that building. Do you understand me?"

"Yes, sir."

Shit. Shit. Shit. She's not stupid and it wouldn't take her long to figure everything out.

Harper

Julius must have told him that he saw me and that I saw him. He's scared now and he'll be heading here. I placed my hand on my belly as I took in a deep breath and waited for Grayson to show up. About fifteen minutes later, the elevator doors opened and the sickness I already felt intensified.

"Harper, I've been trying to call you," he calmly spoke as he walked over to me.

"STOP!" I shouted as I held up my hand from behind. "I have one question for you and you better tell me the truth. Are you Donor 137665?"

Silence momentarily filled the air.

"Yes. I am. Let me explain. Please, sweetheart." He took a step closer, and I jumped up from the stool.

"Don't you ever call me that!" I shouted as I faced him and pointed my finger at him. "You knew all this time that this is your baby and you never told me?" What kind of fucking game are you playing?"

"First, you need to calm down for the baby's sake."

"YOU DON'T GET TO TELL ME TO CALM DOWN!"

"Harper, you're a smart woman and you know you need to calm down."

"I want the truth, Grayson. The whole fucking truth. NOW!" I screamed.

"I'll tell you everything but please just go sit down on the couch."

I inhaled a deep breath as I walked into the living room and he followed behind. I took a seat while he paced back and forth across the room.

"It all started with a stupid bet between me and Julius. If I lost, I had to donate my sperm. Which I did lose. He promised me that nothing would come of it and that he just got pleasure out of making me suffer. He told me it would be buried where no one would ever see it for one month and that I had nothing to worry about. Then him and Yasmin left for vacation and somehow my donor information got sent to you. When Julius told me that a woman had purchased my sperm and was pregnant, I flew off the handle. He told me just to forget about it and that I made some woman very happy. Then my grandfather called me to dinner one night and gave me an ultimatum. He didn't agree with the way I was living my life and told me I had one year to find someone and fall in love or else he was going to sign the company over to Alfie instead of me."

"So you used me?" I narrowed my eye at him.

"Just listen to me, please." He took a few steps towards me.

"Don't you dare take another step towards me. I swear to God, Grayson."

"You have no idea how sorry I am for all of this."

"Really? You used me so you could get your grandfather's company, Grayson?"

He took in a sharp breath.

"Let me guess. You had Julius look up the woman who bought your sperm."

"Yes, and I'm totally ashamed. It wasn't his fault. I made him do it. I felt like he owed me for my goddamn sperm getting out there in the first place."

"So what were you going to do once you got your company? Dump me?" Tears started to stream down my face.

"Harper, please. That was the plan but then I fell in love with you. You are the best thing that has ever happened to me."

I wiped the tears that wouldn't stop falling.

"So you knew all this time you're this baby's father, and you were just going to dump both of us like we're nothing? Like we're trash to you?"

"Don't say it like that. I wanted to tell you so many times."

"Then why didn't you?" I shouted as I stood up from the couch.

"Because I couldn't. The last thing I wanted to do was hurt you or the baby. You have to believe me. I love you and that baby so much that it hurts. You changed me, Harper. You've made me a better man. A man who is finally capable of love."

"Bullshit, Grayson! You lied to me every single day we were together. Charlotte was right."

"Right about what?"

"About you. That's why we got into that argument. She never trusted you from day one." I paused for a moment as something hit me. "Oh my God! Julius was the one who delivered the flowers from the center that day. Starbucks wasn't a coincidence, was it? You followed me there."

He looked down as he placed his hands in his pant pockets.

"The job. The apartment. All this time I was nothing but a pawn in your sick little fucking game!"

"That's not true. I love you. It may have started out that way, but I had feelings for you right from the start. The more time we spent together, the more I fell in love with you. You have to believe me."

"I will never believe another word you say again. You are an arrogant piece of shit who doesn't deserve to love or be loved by anyone. You are nothing but a cold and calculating man without any regard for other people's feelings. You hurt me in the worst possible way, and I will never forgive you for that." I swallowed hard. This game is over, Grayson, and you better believe I fucking won it. I hope you rot in Hell."

I grabbed my purse and laptop and pushed the button to the elevator.

"Harper, please." He grabbed hold of my arm and fell to his knees. "Don't leave me. I need you and our daughter. I love you so much."

"This baby is mine and only mine. You signed away your parental rights to this child. I don't ever want my little girl to know what kind of man her father really is."

As soon as the doors opened, I yanked myself out of his grip and stepped inside.

CHAPTER 40

Harper

The only thing I felt was the shattering of my heart. It hurt so bad that I'd swear I was having a heart attack. I sat in the back of the cab on the way to my apartment trying to hold it together the best I could. As soon as he pulled up to my building, I climbed out and watched as Sammy held the door open for me.

"Good to see you, Harper. Mr. Rhodes called looking for you."

"I know, Sammy. You won't be seeing him around here much anymore."

"I'm sorry to hear that. Are you okay?" he asked as he pushed the elevator button for me.

"Not really."

"If you need anything. Call me."

"Thank you."

I finally made it to my apartment. The moment I stepped inside and shut the door, I fell to the floor in a fetal position and started sobbing. My phone that was in my purse kept ringing. I ignored it. I stayed curled up on the floor for what seemed like hours. My door opened and Charlotte and Laurel came running in.

"Oh my God, Harper. Are you okay?" Charlotte asked.

"Harper, what happened?" Laurel placed her hand on my shoulder.

"We tried calling you and when you didn't answer we got worried, so we came over," Charlotte said.

"Tell us what happened. Is it the baby? Do we need to call 911?" Laurel asked.

I slowly shook my head.

"It's Grayson. It's over."

"Shit," Charlotte spoke. "Come on, let's get you up and on the couch and you can tell us about it."

"I can't. I don't want to move. I can't move."

"Yes, you can, sweetie," Laurel said as her and Charlotte grabbed my arms, helped me up and walked me over to the couch.

"I'm going to make some hot tea," she said as she walked into the kitchen.

"Harper, what happened?" Charlotte asked as she brushed the strands of hair from my face.

"You were right about him all along. He was only using me to get his company."

"What? I don't understand."

Laurel walked in and handed me my cup of tea.

"The baby." I could barely speak.

"What about the baby?" Laurel asked.

"Grayson's the father. He's Donor 137665. And his best friend, Julius is the Director of the cryobank. He said he lost a bet and he had to donate his sperm, but Julius promised nothing would happen with it. But somehow someone screwed up and sent his profile to me. Then his grandfather gave him an ultimatum. He told him he had a year to find someone and fall in love or else he was signing the company over to someone else."

"That fucking asshole," Charlotte said.

"So he sought me out. The woman who purchased his sperm."

"And what the fuck was he planning on doing once he got his company?" Laurel asked.

I looked at both of them as the tears started flowing again.

"I'll kill him," Charlotte snapped.

"He begged me to forgive him. He said that he fell in love with me and wanted to tell me so many times, but he didn't want to hurt me. You should have seen him. He was on his knees begging me not to leave, and he told me I changed him."

"Doesn't matter. I'm still going to kill him," Charlotte said.

"I can't believe I'm going to say this, but I do believe he loves you, Harper," Laurel said.

"WTF, Laurel!" Charlotte snapped.

"I'm just saying when I see them together, I notice the way he looks at her. There was no pretending going on there. What he did was wrong and unforgivable, but I do believe he loves you, Harper."

"God, I'm going to fucking kill him! I told you, Harper. I told you something was up with him!" Charlotte spoke.

"Now's not the time," Laurel said.

"I just want to go to bed."

"Of course. Come on." They helped me up.

"Listen, Harper. You can't stress out about this," Charlotte said. "It's not good for the baby. You have to think about the baby. You don't need to be going into labor."

"I know. I love him so much and I don't know how I'll get over this."

"We'll be here to help you, sweetie," Laurel said.

"Thank you for coming over, but I just really want to be alone right now."

"Call us if you need anything. I don't have a client until eleven o'clock tomorrow, so I'll be by in the morning," Charlotte said.

"And I'll be by after work," Laurel spoke. "Speaking of work, what are you going to do?"

"I'm quitting. There's no way I'll work for that man. I guess I'll have to text him and tell him."

"Where's your phone?" Charlotte asked. "I'll do it for you."

"In my purse."

After sending Grayson a text message, she left my phone on the nightstand and the both of them left. I lay there and cried myself to sleep.

CHAPTER 41

Grayson

I threw my glass at the wall as it shattered all over the floor. Then I took another glass and threw that as anger consumed me.

"Whoa," Julius said as he walked in. "Grayson, calm the fuck down."

"I can't. God, Julius, you should have seen her. I've never felt so much pain in my life. What the fuck am I going to do?"

"There's nothing you can do. You lied to her for months, Grayson. I warned you about this."

"I love her so much. You don't understand. I can't live without her and my daughter."

"Then you're going to have to try and win her back. But to be honest, I don't think she'll take you back. Not to mention she's probably going to sue the fuck out of the cryobank."

"She won't do that."

"You can't be so sure about that."

"I know her, and she won't."

"You know her when she's stable. God knows the mental state she's in now. You fucked that poor woman up. She loved you, man."

"You don't think I know that," I spoke through gritted teeth as I grabbed his shirt.

"Don't. Don't you dare yell at me. You're the one who wanted to get involved to make sure you got your company. I hope it was worth it. You destroyed that poor woman's life; the mother of your child."

"She told me she never wants my daughter to know what kind of man I really am."

"I'm sorry, bro. I really am."

"If you don't mind, I want to be alone."

"Sure." He patted my shoulder. "Call me if you need anything."

One Month Later

For the past month, I sent her a dozen roses every day with a card telling her how sorry I was and that I loved her. I tried to send her some text messages, but they wouldn't go through. I was sure she blocked my number. I hadn't been in the office much and did a lot of work from home. The past couple of weeks, I told Christine that I was sick with the flu. I couldn't bear to leave the penthouse anymore. All I did was drink and sleep. I hated myself for what I'd done. I had never felt so low my entire life. I couldn't do this anymore. The pain of being here in the city was killing me.

I had Damon drive me to my grandfather's house because I needed to tell him. He had been in Florida and didn't know what happened. He was going to be so pissed, but I didn't care anymore.

"Grayson, you look like shit," he said as he walked into the living room. "Are you still sick?"

"No. I need to talk to you."

"Sit down. What is it?"

"I've done something really bad. Something I can't take back."

"What did you do?"

I closed my eyes and took in a deep breath.

"Me and Harper are no longer together. She left me because I lied to her."

"Good God, Grayson. What did you lie about?"

"I made a bet with Julius a couple of years ago and I lost. Because I lost, I had to donate some of my sperm to the cryobank where Julius works. My profile was never to be found or seen, but somehow when he and Yasmin were on vacation, it did, and it was sent to Harper. She chose me and became pregnant."

"What? Are you telling me that you're the father of Harper's baby after you sat here and told me you weren't?"

"Yes. After you gave me that ultimatum, I found out who she was, and I pursued her. My plan was to make you believe that I loved her and when you signed over the company to me, I was going to break it off. But then I fell in love with her." Tears started to stream down my face. "I wanted to tell her so many times what I'd done but I couldn't. I couldn't bear to hurt her. I loved her too much." I cried. "She found out and now she's gone. She told me she never wanted to see me again."

My grandfather sat there and stared at me without saying a word. I was waiting for his wrath and I was prepared for it. Nothing more could bring me down any lower than I already was. I had totally hit rock bottom.

"What you did was wrong and now you're receiving your punishment for it. I'm not going to say anything else to you because the pain and suffering of losing someone you love is bad enough. Especially when it was done out of betrayal. You reap what you sow, son. I'm very disappointed in you."

"I know you are and I'm sorry. I swear to you that if I could take it all back, I would in a heartbeat. And this is why I need to do what I came here to do."

"And what is that?"

"I quit. You can hand the company over to Alfie. I'm sure he'll do a great job."

"So you're giving it all up?"

"I am. My greed and the need for power was what led all of this to happen. If I can't have Harper and my daughter by my side while I'm running the company, then I don't want it. I'm sorry, Grandfather. I'm truly sorry for everything I've done."

I walked out and climbed into the back of the Escalade.

"What did he say?" Damon asked.

"Nothing. He barely said anything at all."

CHAPTER 42

Harper

The past month had been the worst weeks of my life. I'd barely left the apartment and I did nothing but cry and sleep. I was sitting on the couch scrolling through my pictures when I came across the one of us at Belvedere's Castle. Tears started to stream down my face once again.

There was a knock at the door and when I opened it, Sammy stood there holding another dozen red roses.

"Oh my God. This is ridiculous."

"He's trying to make you see how sorry he is."

"I don't care, Sammy. Take them. Give them to your wife and do me a favor, if any more come, don't bring them up. I don't want anything from that man. In fact, refuse the delivery."

"If that's what you want."

"I do. It's exactly what I want."

I was almost thirty-three weeks pregnant and I had just started on the nursery. Laurel and Charlotte offered to help but I wanted to do it on my own. Being out of work for the past month had taken a toll on my savings account. I still had quite a bit of money saved, but the rent was almost due and there was a crib I desperately wanted that cost fifteen hundred dollars. I knew it was pricey, but I didn't care. It was for my baby and she deserved nothing but the best. I sat down at the table and pulled up my bank account while I ate breakfast. My brows furrowed as I saw the balance in my account. What the hell? That isn't right. The bank must have made an error and keyed in a wrong number when a deposit was made. I had to run out to the store, so I'd stop by the bank and make them aware of their error.

"May I help you?" A perky blonde behind the counter asked.

"There's been an error in my bank account."

"Okay. Can I see your I.D. please?"

I reached in my wallet, pulled out my I.D. and handed it to her. She fiercely started typing away on her keyboard.

"What error are you referring to?"

"Um. The five hundred-thousand-dollar deposit that was made. I didn't make that deposit. I'm sure whoever entered it hit a wrong number. It needs to be straightened out ASAP so the person who it belongs to gets their money."

"Hmm. Let me check. Nope. There is no error. That money was transferred into your account."

"I'm sorry but you must be mistaken."

"Honey, I'm looking at the deposit slip here. It has your account number on it."

"Who deposited that money into my account? Wait. Never mind." I shook my head. "I'm sorry to have wasted your time."

"No problem. Can I offer you a piece of advice? Someone wanted you to have that money. Consider yourself lucky. I'd kill for someone to deposit that into my account." She grinned.

I gave her a fake smile and walked out of the bank. I was fuming. How dare he. I wanted nothing from him. Especially his fucking money. I pulled out my phone and did a three-way call with Charlotte and Laurel.

"You are never going to believe this?"

"What happened?" They both asked at the same time.

"Grayson deposited five hundred thousand dollars into my bank account."

"Good. What's the problem?" Charlotte asked.

"I don't want his money! I want nothing from him ever again."

"Harper, he's making sure you and the baby are financially okay. Take the damn money and forget where it came from. It's the least he can do after what he did to you," Laurel spoke.

"I can't."

"Yes, you can. You're five hundred thousand dollars richer. Who the fuck cares where it came from? Treat yourself," Charlotte said.

I sighed as I placed my phone back in my purse. Was this his attempt to try and make me forgive him? Because if it was, he failed.

CHAPTER 43

Harper
I was walking down Park Avenue and stopped in front of the high-rise that was being built. The one I designed. Staring at it, tears started to fill my eyes.

"Can I help you, lady?" one of the workers asked.

"No. I'm just admiring the building."

"Pretty cool, huh?"

"Yeah. Seeing it from the model to actually being almost built is kind of surreal."

"Do you work for the company?"

"I did. I was the one who designed this building."

"Wow. Really? Congratulations."

"Thank you." I gave him a small smile.

"I gotta get back to work. Have a nice day."

"You too."

I wiped the tear that fell down my cheek and headed home.

The nursery was complete. I'd painted the walls a light grey and bought all white furniture. The one piece I loved the most was the crib with tufted pink fabric on each end. It was elegant and made for a princess. Her name sat above it in big pink letters. I'd painted the ceiling a lighter shade of gray and added white fluffy clouds and stars painted white with a hint of light pink giving off a beautiful glow. As I stood back with my hand on my belly and admired it, a call came in from the lobby.

"Hello."

"Harper, it's Sammy. There's a Mr. Rhodes Sr. here to see you."

My belly started to twist in knots. Grayson's grandfather? Why would he be here?

"Send him up. Thanks, Sammy."

I walked over to the door and opened it just as he stepped off the elevator.

"Mr. Rhodes. What are you doing here?"

"Hello, Harper. May I come in?"

"Of course."

"Thank you. My, look at you." He smiled. "How much longer do you have?"

"Four weeks left."

"You look as beautiful as ever." He leaned in and kissed my cheek.

"Can I offer you some tea or coffee?"

"Coffee would be nice. Thank you."

I went into the kitchen and made us each a cup of coffee. When I went to hand him his cup, I couldn't find him. So I walked down the hallway and saw him standing in the nursery.

"Forgive me." He smiled. "I just wanted to see where my great granddaughter was going to be sleeping."

"He told you?"

"Yes. Grayson told me everything. Let's go sit down."

We walked to the dining area and took a seat at the table.

"Ever since Grayson's parents passed away, he wasn't the same. He was reckless in his youth which continued into his adult years, but he had a good business sense. He knew how to separate his business life from his personal life."

"I'm sorry, Mr. Rhodes, but why are you telling me this?"

He held up his finger as he sipped his coffee.

"What Grayson did was awful, but I am to blame for that. I was the one who gave him that ultimatum. I believe I failed him in many ways. I was never going to sign the company over to Alfie. I'd just said that to scare a little sense into Grayson to want to get his personal life together. At the rate he was going, he would never have found true love. I figured if I could get him to be serious and give a woman more than one chance, he would find it and see how beautiful life could be when you have someone to share it with. Unfortunately, he went about it the wrong way. But he learned his lesson the hard way. He loves you, Harper, and he loves that baby. So much so that he quit and told me he didn't want the company."

"What?" I cocked my head.

"He came to me and told me that if he couldn't run the company without you and his daughter by his side, he didn't want it. So he quit and now he's gone."

"Gone where?"

"Nobody knows. He just up and left." He sighed.

"Did you ask, Julius?"

"Yes, and he said he didn't know, and that Grayson never even told him he was leaving. He gave everything up because he lost you. I'm not telling you any of this to make you feel bad or sorry for him. Because what he did to you was terrible. But I want you to try and take some comfort that he does truly love you and he didn't lie about that."

"Thank you, Mr. Rhodes."

"Please, darling, call me Leon. Will you please keep in touch with me? I would love to meet my great granddaughter when she's born."

"Yes. I promise I will."

He got up from his seat and walked to the door.

"I can see why Grayson chose you, Harper. You're an amazing woman, and you will be an amazing mother. Have a good day."

"Thank you, Leon."

I shut the door and took in a deep breath. I went about my day and tried to put everything Leon said out of my mind. Grayson giving up his company was huge, and I couldn't imagine him doing that. He loved that company more than anything. I tossed and turned all night long and I barely slept.

A couple days had passed, and I couldn't stop thinking about Leon's visit. It was a constant gnawing inside of me. Fuck it! I took a cab over to the cryobank and went up to Julius's office.

"Harper?" he spoke in shock. "What are you doing here?"

"Hello, Julius." I arched my brow at him.

"Have a seat." He gestured.

"I need you to tell me where Grayson is."

"I have no clue."

"Bullshit. You two are attached at the hip. There's no way Grayson would leave without telling you where he was going."

"Seriously, Harper, I don't know."

"Listen to me." I got up from my chair and planted my finger on his desk as my face was mere inches from his. "You don't want to mess with a pregnant lady. You had no problem telling him that I was the one who bought his sperm creating this clusterfuck of a mess. A mess in which I should sue your ass and this company for. Now where the fuck is Grayson?!"

He sat there, leaning as far back from me as possible.

"He's in Montauk. Let me get you the address." He grabbed a pen and a piece of paper, wrote the address down and handed it to me.

"Thank you."

As I walked to the door and placed my hand on the handle, Julius called my name.

"Harper."

"What?" I turned my head.

"He's changed and he doesn't look the same. I just want to give you a heads up."

"Thanks. Have a nice day."

I looked up the distance online and it was about a two hour and forty-five-minute drive. I packed a small bag just in case I needed it and rented a car. While I was driving, I called both Laurel and Charlotte to let them know I would be out of town for a couple days, but I didn't tell them where I was going.

"I don't understand why you're leaving town," Charlotte asked.

"I just need to get away for a couple of days. The baby will be here in four weeks and I just need some time alone to think and do some soul searching."

"You better be careful, Harper," Laurel said.

"I will. I just need a change of scenery."

CHAPTER 44

Harper

I slammed on my breaks and stopped at the entrance of what appeared to be a driveway. According to my GPS, this is where the house was located but I didn't see a house. I turned into the driveway which ended up being a long winding road that led straight to a two-story gray sided home that sat a few feet away from the sandy beach. I gripped the steering wheel as I began questioning why I even came here. He was no longer my problem. I nervously climbed out of the car and stepped onto the porch, lightly knocking on the door as my heart raced a mile a minute. I knocked again and there was no answer. Maybe he wasn't home. I looked around and there wasn't another house around as far as the eye could see. By the looks of it, this would be considered a hideaway home, secluded by hills and trees.

Walking around the back, I noted the cobblestone path that led down to the beach. I stood there and stared at the magnificent view of the ocean as a cool wind swept across my face. I was snapped back into reality when I heard footsteps. Turning around, I saw a man I didn't recognize.

"Harper? What are you doing here? How did you know where to

find me?" Grayson asked in a flat tone as he held two brown bags in his arms. "Let me guess, Julius?"

I stared at him for a moment. His face enshrouded by a full beard and mustache. His hair was longer than normal, and he was dressed in jeans and a gray flannel button up shirt.

"He had no choice. I threatened to sue him."

Grayson turned around and opened the side door without saying a word. I ran up to the door and stepped inside as he set the bags on the island in the kitchen.

"You didn't answer my question. What are you doing here?"

"What happened to you?" I asked as I stared at him.

"Life. That's what. You shouldn't have come. Heavy rains are headed this way soon and there's a chance the roads could wash out. It isn't safe for you here. Go back to the city," he spoke as he pulled his groceries from the bags.

"I'll take my chances. Your grandfather paid me a little visit a couple days ago. He said you quit and told him to sign the company over to Alfie because you didn't want it."

"Did he now? He shouldn't have told you that."

"So what? Is this your new life now? Hiding away from your family and friends? Giving up your dream of owning the company? Something you worked so hard for."

"I'm not that man anymore. The company doesn't matter to me."

"And why do you look like a lumberjack?"

He shot me a look and shook his head.

"Is this why you came all the way out here? To insult me and my decisions?"

Suddenly the winds picked up, the sky opened, and heavy rain started to pelt against the windows.

"Shit," he said.

"No. I don't know why I came out here to be honest," I spoke as I crossed my arms and stared at the pouring down rain from the window. Shit was right. I was going to be stuck here for a while.

"You shouldn't have come, Harper."

"Well, it's a little too late for that. Isn't it?"

I walked around and looked at the interior of the home. The light beige walls, the dark wood flooring and the large beige area rugs that were scattered throughout the house. The one thing that caught my attention was the 30 ft. high stone fireplace and the grand piano that sat next to it in the corner.

"This place is really nice. Are you renting it?"

"No. It's mine. I bought it." He walked over to the bar and poured himself a drink. "This place was our vacation home when I was a kid."

"You still had it after all these years?"

"No. I just bought it about three months ago. I was looking for a house to buy as a summer home for us." He looked away. "Then this popped up and I had no choice. I had to buy it."

"You bought this for us?" I narrowed my eye at him. "Don't you mean for you? Because your plan was to dump me once you got your company."

"It doesn't matter anymore, and I really don't want to discuss it."

I went to the refrigerator and pulled out a bottle of water.

"Yes, Grayson, I would like some water." I rolled my eyes as I took a seat on the couch.

"Sorry. I'm still in shock you're here."

"Me too. So now what? Obviously, I can't go anywhere."

"Are you hungry? I can fix us some dinner."

I couldn't help but let out a laugh.

"You can't cook."

"I've been managing just fine." He walked into the kitchen.

"I can't believe how hard it's raining," I spoke.

"I told you heavy rains were coming. Did you think I was lying?"

"It wouldn't be the first time."

He shot me a look and slowly shook his head.

"Okay. Since I'm stuck here, I hate just standing around. At least let me help you cook."

"You should go rest for a while. You look tired."

"I don't want to rest. I want to help."

"I'm making chili. If you want to help so bad, then you can make a salad. You'll find everything in the refrigerator."

I opened the fridge and took out lettuce, cucumbers and tomatoes. Taking a knife from the knife block, I began to cut up the lettuce on a cutting board that was already on the counter. Silence filled the space between us. He was the one who deceived me and yet I was the one getting an attitude from him.

"Do you have a bowl I can put this salad in?" I asked.

"In that cabinet over there." He pointed.

I made the salad as he continued making the chili.

"Do you mind if I take a taste?"

"Why? Don't you trust my ability?" His brow raised.

"No. Actually, I don't."

"Be my guest." He handed me a wooden spoon.

"Needs a little more spice."

"Then spice it up." He handed me the chili powder.

As I was spicing up the chili, he set the table. I couldn't believe this was happening. As soon as the chili was ready, we took our seats at the table.

"You're not going to be able to leave tonight so you'll have to sleep in one of the guest rooms. There's three of them so take your pick."

All of a sudden, the house went dark. The only light was from the fire that was roaring in the fireplace.

"Shit!" he said. "Don't move. I'll go turn on the generator."

This was just dandy as fuck. Here I was stuck in a house, having dinner with a man I never wanted to see again, in the middle of a storm and the power goes out.

CHAPTER 45

Grayson

I couldn't believe she was here. Seeing her hurt all over again. She looked just as beautiful now as she did the day everything changed. She was way bigger with a bigger attitude. Hell, I didn't blame her. But she still never fully said why she came here.

I could barely look at her. Every time I did, it reminded me of what I'd done and how badly I hurt her. I came to Montauk because nobody here knew who I was, and I wanted to put the past behind me. To make a fresh start.

After turning on the generator, I took my seat at the table and continued to eat my dinner.

"So what do you do here all day?" she asked.

"I've been working on the house. It needed a bit of updating."

"Oh. I didn't know you could do things like that."

"I learned."

"I have a question for you, and I want an honest answer," she spoke.

"What?" I looked straight at her.

"Why did you deposit that money into my bank account?"

"For you and the baby."

"Did you think you could just buy your way back into our lives?"

"Damn it, Harper!" I slammed my fist on the table and got up from my chair. "That's not why I did it. You quit your job!"

"Yeah, because of you!" she shouted.

"I know that. I know that I'm one hundred percent responsible for that. But I want to make sure you and my daughter are taken care of without you having to worry about finances. It's the least I could do after what I'd done." I turned away and threw my bowl in the sink.

"Why, Grayson? How could you do that to me?"

I placed my hands on the counter and looked down.

"Because I let my fears get the best of me. When my parents died, I suddenly had all this fear. I acted out, I rebelled. You name it, I did it. Don't get me wrong, my grandparents were good to me and raised me the best they could, but they weren't my parents. I felt like I'd lost everything when they died. Almost as if a part of me died with them. I couldn't control what happened to them, but I could do my best to control my own life. I felt the need for such control out of the fear that consumed me. And it was that same fear that led me to do what I did. I know you don't believe me, but I'm not that man anymore, and I have you to thank for that. I don't ever expect you to forgive me. Hell, I don't deserve your forgiveness, nor will I ever forgive myself for what I'd done to you."

※

Harper

"You act like you're the fucking victim here, Grayson."

"I'm not the victim, Harper, nor do I pretend to be. You wanted to know why, and I told you. If me telling you the truth isn't good enough, then I'm sorry. I'm going upstairs. Take whichever guest room you want," he spoke as he began to walk away.

I got up from the chair, took a few steps and froze as a pain tore through me and I felt something warm travel down my legs.

"Grayson," I spoke in a panicked tone.

He stopped, turned around, looked at the ground and then up at me.

"I think my water just broke. Oh god." I clutched my belly.

"Shit," he said as he ran over to me and grabbed hold of my arm. "Come on. Let's get you to the couch."

"No. I'm soaking wet."

"Just sit down in the chair for a minute. I'll run upstairs and get you one of my shirts. I promise I'll be back in a second. Okay?"

I nodded my head as I sat down. Within a moment, he was back with one of his t-shirts. One I used to wear all the time before I had kept extra clothes at his house. He helped me from the chair and into the bathroom.

"Let me help you change out of those clothes," he said.

"No. I can do it. I think you better call 911."

"Right. I'll go grab my phone."

I stripped out of my clothes and slipped on his t-shirt. This wasn't happening and I started to panic. When I walked out of the bathroom, I went and sat down on the couch. Suddenly, another cramping pain fired through me.

"Oh my God!"

"They're sending an ambulance as soon as they can, but the roads are washed out and they don't know how long it will take for them to get here."

"It's too early, Grayson. I'm not due for another four weeks. I can't have her yet. It's too soon." I grabbed his arm.

"Shh. It'll be okay. Everything will be okay. I will not let anything happen to you or the baby. They'll be here."

CHAPTER 46

Grayson

Two hours had passed, and the ambulance still wasn't here. Harper's contractions were coming closer together and as much as I wanted to panic, I couldn't. I needed to be strong for her. All I could see was the fear in her eyes. She was scared shitless and so was I. I placed a blanket on the floor with a bunch of pillows and I held her from behind as she sat in between my legs. Her contractions were now four minutes apart and with each one, she let out a howling scream.

My phone rang. I quickly answered it and put it on speaker.

"Hello."

"This is Dr. Graham. Whom am I speaking with?"

"Grayson Rhodes. I'm with Harper Holland and we're in Montauk. Her water broke, and she's in labor."

"You need to get her to a hospital immediately."

"I would if I could, but we're in the middle of a horrific storm and the roads are washed out. I called 911 and they're sending an ambulance but that was two hours ago and they're still not here."

"Harper, can you hear me?"

"Yes. Dr. Graham. Oh God," she screamed.

"Mr. Rhodes, how far apart are her contractions?"

"About three to four minutes apart."

"Okay. Mr. Rhodes, you're going to have to deliver this baby. Harper, I want you to listen to me and I want you to remain as calm as possible. Your body knows exactly what to do."

"Dr. Graham, it's too early to have her."

"Harper, everything is going to be okay. Mr. Rhodes, I want you to go get some towels, a blanket and a cool cloth for Harper's head."

"No. Don't leave me," she begged as she grabbed my arm.

"I'll be right back. You have my word."

I got up and quickly grabbed a blanket, some towels and a cool cloth like Dr. Graham said. Harper screamed out in pain.

"I have to push."

"Not yet, Harper," Dr. Graham said. "Practice your breathing."

"Oh God!" she screamed.

"Dr. Graham. Her contractions are two minutes apart now."

"Okay. Let's do this. Harper, I want you to push with the next contraction. Mr. Rhodes, you need to tell me when you start to see the baby's head."

I held Harper's hand as the next few contractions hit, and she pushed as she screamed in pain.

"I see it, Dr. Graham. I see her head."

"Okay. I want the next push to be even bigger, Harper."

She pushed as hard as she could and then stopped.

"I can't. I can't do this anymore. She fell back onto the pillows."

I placed my hand on her forehead and stared into her beautiful blue and tired eyes.

"Sweetheart, you have no choice. Our daughter is ready to meet you, but she can't do it alone. She needs you to help her along. Okay?"

"Okay." She nodded as she pushed as hard as she could.

"Dr. Graham, her head is out."

"Excellent. Hold onto her. One final push, Harper. That's all it's going take."

Suddenly, she was out and, in my hands, screaming at the top of her lungs.

I'd never felt so much joy in my entire life as my eyes filled with tears. Looking up, I could see the flashing lights of the ambulance outside.

"The paramedics are here."

"Mr. Rhodes. Place the baby on Harper's chest. The paramedics will cut the cord and deliver the placenta. Congratulations you two."

The front door opened, and the paramedics ran in with the stretcher and their medical bags. I moved out of the way and sat next to Harper, who looked at me with tears in her eyes.

"She's beautiful, Grayson."

"She looks just like her mother." I smiled as I kissed her forehead with tears in my eyes.

The paramedics took the baby, cleaned her up, wrapped her tightly in a blanket and handed her back to Harper.

"We need to get the two of you to the hospital," one of the paramedics spoke.

They placed her and the baby on the stretcher and I climbed in the ambulance with them. The baby was resting peacefully against Harper.

"Have you thought of a name for her yet?" I asked as I softly stroked her forehead.

"Ellie Rae. After my parents. Ellie was my mom's name and Ray was my dad's name. But I'm going to spell it Rae."

"It's a beautiful name." I smiled.

The moment we arrived at the hospital, they took Ellie to the NICU and put Harper in a room. I stayed by her side the entire time, refusing to leave her.

"Thank you, Grayson." She held her hand out to me. "I couldn't have done it without you."

I gave her a smile as I gently squeezed her hand.

"Harper," An older man in a long white coat walked into the room. "Your daughter is doing fine. She's a little jaundice which is normal so we're keeping her under the heat lamps overnight and monitoring her. Otherwise, she's healthy."

Both Harper and I let out a sigh of relief.

"I'm staying here with you, whether you want me to or not," I said to her.

"I was hoping you'd stay."

After Harper fell asleep, I laid down on the couch in the room. It wasn't the most comfortable couch, but I was exhausted, and I had no trouble falling asleep.

CHAPTER 47

Harper

I awoke the next morning as the sun was out and drying up all the chaos from last night. I looked over at the couch and smiled when I saw Grayson sleeping. The nurse walked in pushing a hospital bassinet that held my baby girl.

"It's time for her feeding, Mom." The nurse smiled as she picked her up and handed her to me.

Grayson woke up and sat on the edge of the bed while I fed her.

"She has your nose," I said.

"And she has your lips." He smiled as he placed his finger under her hand and she immediately grasped it.

"I need to go home and change. But I'll be back as soon as possible."

"Of course, go. We'll be fine." I smiled. "Oh my gosh, I have to call Charlotte and Laurel."

"Do you want to use my phone?" he asked.

"No. I can wait. Can you bring my phone and my bag in the car? It's in the back seat."

"One bag and a phone. Got it." He grinned. "I'll be back as soon as I can."

"Wait. Can you also bring me back a burger and some fries?" I bit down on my bottom lip.

"One burger and fries coming right up." He winked as he walked out of the room.

"Is that Ellie's father?" the nurse asked as she walked in.

"Yes." I smiled. "He is her father."

◈

After I fed Ellie, I set her down in her crib so I could fill out the paperwork the hospital gave me. About three hours had passed and Grayson still wasn't back. Thoughts that he was never coming back filled my head. No. He wouldn't do that. But what the hell was taking him so long?

"Did someone order a burger and fries?" He smiled as he held up a brown bag.

I stared at him in shock. His hair was cut, and his face was shaven clean except for a hint of stubble that shrouded his masculine jawline.

"Look at you." I smiled. "You clean up pretty good, Mr. Rhodes."

"I couldn't have my daughter thinking I looked like a lumberjack, could I? Here's your burger and fries. I'm sorry it took so long but I had to do a little shopping."

"Shopping? For what?"

He stepped out into the hallway and rolled in a cart.

"Flowers for the beautiful new mother." He handed me a bouquet of red roses.

"Thank you. They're beautiful."

"I picked up some diapers, a car seat, and some outfits. I actually couldn't decide what I liked best, so I just bought them all."

"Oh my God," I laughed as he pulled out all kinds of newborn outfits from the bag. "It looks like you bought out the whole store."

"Trust me, the sales lady was very happy with my purchase."

"Do you want to hold her?" I asked.

"Can I?"

"Yes. Just pick her up."

He carefully picked her up out of the crib and sat down in the rocking chair next to the bed. As I ate my burger and fries, I watched him stare at her. He wouldn't take his eyes off her as he stroked her little hand. I could see the love he had for her just by his expression. It was then I knew I'd made the right decision.

"I had to fill out the birth certificate. Can you make sure I did it right?" I asked as I handed the form to him.

He took it from me, read it over and then looked up at me with tears in his eyes.

"Ellie Rae Rhodes. You gave her my last name?"

"You did deliver her. You were the one who made sure she came into the world safely. And, you are her father. So it's only right that she has your name."

"Harper, I—"

"Don't, Grayson. Let's just leave it at that for now."

༶

I was discharged the following day. I had called Laurel and Charlotte and they couldn't believe it when I told them that I had the baby and that Grayson was the one who delivered her. They were so shocked, for once in their lives, they were speechless.

"I'm going to drive you back to the city and I don't want any arguments," he said.

"That's fine. You won't get any argument from me."

"Really?" His brow arched.

"Yes. I'm too tired to drive. Grayson, listen, I want you to come back with me. The city is where you belong. This place is amazing and the perfect summer home, but there's nothing here for you."

"What's back in the city for me?"

"Ellie? Your company?"

"Harper, I'm not going back there. I can't."

"You can. You claim you're a changed man. Then show me. That company is yours. It's what you love."

"There are other things I love more. That company destroyed me."

"No, Grayson, your need for power and greed is what destroyed you."

"We better get you and Ellie back to the city," he spoke. "Just let me pack a few things first."

CHAPTER 48

Grayson

I secured Ellie's car seat in the back of my SUV and arranged for someone to pick up the rental car and return it. Harper sat in the back, never taking her eyes off our daughter. This reminded me of when I was a child. Sometimes on our way back from Montauk, my mother would sit in the backseat with me and she'd either read to me or we'd play silly games.

Harper told me I had Ellie, but she didn't say I had her, and I would not push it. She was right. It was my need for power and greed that destroyed me. I wasn't that man anymore. Damon once told me that there was more to life than a high-powered company and money, and he was right.

I pulled up to her apartment building, helped Harper out of the SUV and then grabbed Ellie's car seat. Sammy held the door open with a wide grin across his face.

"Harper. Mr. Rhodes. It's good to see you both. And who do we have here?"

"Sammy, I'd like you to meet Ellie Rae Rhodes." Harper grinned.

"So, Mr. Rhodes, is her father?" he asked in confusion.

"Yes. It's a long story, Sammy, but I am Ellie's father."

"That's wonderful news. She's beautiful."

"Thank you, Sammy. One day I'll tell you the story." Harper grinned as we took the elevator up to her apartment.

"Oh, Sammy. There are some bags in the car. Can you get them for us and send them up?"

"Of course, Mr. Rhodes." He nodded.

The moment we stepped inside her apartment, I set Ellie's car seat on the table. She was sound asleep and looked like an absolute angel.

"I want to show you something," Harper spoke as she took hold of my hand and led me to the nursery.

"Wow. Did you do all this?"

"I did. What do you think of the ceiling?"

"It's perfect. A room that is truly fit for a princess." I smiled.

"Can you watch her for me while I take a quick shower?" she asked.

"Yes, of course I will."

Harper went into the bathroom and I unbuckled Ellie from her car seat, carefully picked her up and took her over to the couch.

"My darling princess. Once upon a time, there was this beautiful woman who wanted nothing more than a family of her own. One day, she set out to make that happen and after it did, she met a man. A man who at first didn't want the same things she did. But the more time he spent with her, the more he fell in love with her. This woman was so beautiful and kind-hearted that anyone who met her instantly fell in love with her. She showed the man the beauty of true love. She melted his frozen heart and showed him there was so much more to life than just work. She brightened up his dismal days and brought the man to life. This beautiful woman was the most amazing person the man ever met. She's your mom, and you are incredibly lucky to have her. I've never loved anyone in my life the way I love her and you, my beautiful daughter. My angel. I promise that I will protect you, guide you, and be there for you when you're down. I will never be too busy for you. You have my word. The only thing that matters in my life, are you and your mother, and I pray that someday she will forgive me for what I'd done and the pain I caused her."

Harper

I stood around the corner and listened to every word he said as tears filled my eyes. Even after everything that happened, I still loved him. I went into the bedroom and slipped into a pair of leggings and an oversized sweatshirt.

"Hey," Grayson spoke as he stepped inside. "Did you call Laurel and Charlotte to let them know you and Ellie are home?"

"Not yet."

"I can go if you want," he said.

I turned my head and looked at him.

"Can you stay a while longer?"

"I can stay for as long as you need me to. I do have to make a phone call, though." He stepped out of the room.

I quietly followed him and listened as he called The Plaza Hotel and booked a suite. Why the hell was he doing that?

"Why did you book a suite at the hotel?" I asked.

He turned and looked at me as he placed his phone in his pocket.

"I rented out the penthouse for a year."

"What?" I cocked my head at him. "Why would you do that?"

"Because I didn't have any plans on coming back here, so there was no need to keep it."

"Call the hotel and cancel your suite. You can stay with me until you find another permanent place. I'll need help with Ellie and you're her father, so it's only right that you help me with her."

"Harper—"

"Nope." I put up my hand. "You're staying here. You can sleep on the couch. Got it?"

"Yes. I got it. But I'm sure your friends won't be happy about that."

"I don't give a shit. It's none of their business. You're Ellie's father. If they don't like it, then they don't need to come over. Now if you'll excuse me, I have to go blow dry my hair."

One Week Later

Without Grayson knowing, I called his grandfather to come over so the two of them could talk and he could meet his great granddaughter. Laurel and Charlotte were shocked that I was letting Grayson stay here but they knew better than to say anything about it.

I was in the kitchen when there was knock at the door.

"Who could that be?" Grayson asked.

"I don't know. Can you find out?"

He walked over and opened the door.

"Grandfather. What are you doing here?"

"It's good to see you, Grayson." He gave him a hug. "Harper called and told me that I had to come and meet my great granddaughter. Now, where is she?"

"She's right here?" I smiled as I brought Ellie over to him.

"Harper, she's beautiful. And look at you. You look like you were never even pregnant."

"Thank you. You're too kind. Would you like to hold her?"

"Of course."

"Grandfather, go sit down on the couch and we'll hand her to you."

"Grayson, I've had children and a grandchild. I know how to hold a baby."

I laughed as I handed Ellie over to him.

CHAPTER 49

Grayson

I smiled as I watched my grandfather with her. I'd never seen this side of him before. He was talking to her in a childlike voice. He handed her over to Harper and asked me to sit down. Harper took Ellie into the bedroom and left the two of us alone.

"I have something for you," he spoke as he pulled an envelope out of his coat pocket.

"What is this?"

"Open it and find out."

I opened the envelope, took out the papers, and read them. They were the papers appointing ownership of the company to me.

"Grandfather, I—"

"Stop right there, son. Whether you want it or not, the company is rightfully yours and I expect you to accept it and continue running it the way you had been. Seeing you like this, you remind me so much of your father, and he would be so proud to see what kind of man you turned out to be. Sure, you had a rough patch. Everyone does. But it's how you come back from that is what matters. You were born to take over the family business, and I expect nothing less from you. You can have it all, Grayson. I did and so did your father."

"Grandfather, as much as I'd like to, I just can't."

"For fuck sakes, Grayson, sign the damn papers," Harper snapped as she walked into the room. "Do you honestly think I drove out to Montauk, got stuck in a storm, had our baby on the floor of your house, four weeks early may I add, just for you not to sign those papers. Hell, no! Now you will sign them, and you will go back to work and do what you do best. You will not disappoint me or Ellie. Understand me?"

Grayson stared at me for a moment and then looked at his grandfather.

"I knew I loved this woman." His grandfather smiled.

"Yes, Harper. I understand. Can you get me a pen?"

"I already have one in my hand." She grinned as she handed me the pen and I signed the papers.

After my grandfather left, Harper walked over to me and wrapped her arms around my neck. It had been a long time since she'd done that.

"I'm so proud of you." She smiled. "You did the right thing."

"I don't know. Maybe. Maybe not."

"No. You did. And as for tonight, you're sleeping in my bed, and you're going to hold me, and you're going to get up with Ellie. Understand me?"

"Can I just tell you that you're so sexy when you order me around like that?" I grinned.

"Good. Get used to it."

"Does this mean you forgive me?"

"Not a hundred percent. But I'm getting there." The corners of her mouth curved upward as she pressed her lips against mine.

CHAPTER 50

ONE YEAR LATER

Harper

I stood there in my form fitting, sleeveless white dress that was encased in crystals, kissing the man who was the love of my life and now my husband. I'd never forget the day six months ago, Grayson proposed to me. It was a beautiful sunny day when he took me to Bethesda Terrace in Central Park, got down on one knee and asked me to marry him in the same exact spot where my father had asked my mother. Not only did I spend the last six months planning the perfect wedding, Grayson and I also moved into a gorgeous sixty-five hundred square foot, five-bedroom, six bath townhome on the Upper East Side.

For our honeymoon, we spent a week alone in Bali. As much as we loved our alone time together making love uninterrupted, enjoying great conversation and the beautiful sights, we couldn't wait to get back home to our little girl. So we extended our honeymoon one more week by taking Ellie to Disney World.

Even though she was only a little over a year old, she loved it. She loved meeting all the Disney characters, especially Mickey Mouse. We were walking down the street pushing her in the stroller when she kept pointing and saying "Da-Da."

"Da-Da's right here, princess," Grayson spoke.

"Da-Da." She kept pointing.

Looking over, there stood Cinderella and Prince Charming.

"I think she's pointing at Prince Charming." I laughed.

"Huh?" Grayson looked over.

"Da-Da," Ellie said.

"No way. I'm way better looking than that guy."

"Of course you are, but your daughter sees a prince and thinks it's you. You should be flattered." I smiled as I kissed his lips. "Because you truly are Prince Charming. You're my Prince Charming."

"Thank you. But I'm still better looking than he is." He turned the stroller around, so Prince Charming was out of his daughter's view.

I couldn't help but laugh.

We ate dinner and headed back to the hotel and put Ellie down for the night. The room Grayson got us was a two-bedroom suite in the Grand Floridian Hotel, so we had our own room to ourselves. After making love for the second time that day, I snuggled against him as his arm held me tight.

"I've been thinking about something lately," he said.

"What have you been thinking about?"

"If you're willing, I'd like to have another baby."

"Seriously?" I lifted my head and looked at him with a smile on my face.

"Yes. Seriously. Don't you want one?"

"I do. But I have to ask. How would you like me to get pregnant?"

"Huh?" His brows furrowed.

"Do you want to do it the natural way this time or would you like to make a sperm deposit at the cryobank?"

"Oh, you're hilarious, Harper." He rolled me on my back and hovered over me. "I'm going to make a sperm deposit all right and it won't be through the cryobank. In fact, I'm going to make another one right now." His lips brushed against mine.

"Bring it on, Prince Charming." I grinned.

THE DONOR

One Year Later

*G*rayson

I smiled as I held in my arms, my second daughter, Lily Marie Rhodes, who was named after my mother. She was perfect and born at thirty-eight weeks in a hospital. This birth was easier for Harper since she chose to get plenty of drugs to help her through it. I was a happy man. The company had excelled beyond my expectations. I had an excellent team behind me which freed up my time to spend with my family. I now understood what my grandfather meant about having a family by your side. All three of my girls were the love of my life and I couldn't wait to see what magic the future held for us. Who would have thought my life would have turned out to be so perfect. A life that started out by losing a bet.

*H*arper

I'd finally had the family I'd always dreamed of. The perfect man I'd searched for my entire life and two beautiful children. When I entered the cryobank for the first time, I never thought this is how my life would end up. I never thought Donor 137665 would turn out to be the perfect man and father who would make all my dreams come true.

THEN YOU HAPPENED

PROLOGUE

*D*o you remember when you played with your Barbies as a child? You had a beautiful, blonde-haired Barbie doll that you dressed in the most elegant dress because Ken, the hottest male doll ever made, was coming to pick her up and take her to the most magnificent ball. She'd be up in her room, in the townhouse, looking at herself in the full-length mirror. While butterflies stirred, Barbie would be all giddy with excitement for her date with Ken. The doorbell rang and Barbie would take the elevator down to find Ken, who was looking hot and sexy in his black tuxedo. He would lean in closer for a kiss and whisper in her ear, "Barbie, I'm going to marry you and buy you a dream house where the two of us can raise a happy family."

Barbie would smile at Ken as she jumped up and down in excitement, but still waited for that ring on her finger. She would hook her arm in his and off they would go to the ball.

Once they arrived, Barbie would look around and thank Ken for bringing her to such a glamorous event. She would feel like the luckiest Barbie on Earth to be on the arm of the most handsome male of them all. Barbie was a queen and Ken was her king.

All would go well until Teresa Barbie showed up at the ball with her long, silky, black hair and eyes like a cat. Her skin glowing with a luminous tan as she strutted her little body in her silvery, short, glittered dress past my king. I watched as his head turned and the smile on his face grew wide.

"Excuse me, Barbie. I'm going to get us some drinks from the bar."

He walked away and I noticed he approached Teresa. Tears filled my eyes as I watched them talk and laugh. He grabbed her hand and off they went. My king, stolen by another woman. I ran back to my townhouse, as my world was now shattered. The love of my life. My king. My Ken, dumped me for another Barbie. My life would never be the same.

And that was where it all began. Somehow, we knew, even as children who played innocently with Barbies, that men would ultimately betray us and fill our hearts with promises they never intended to keep, leaving us alone and wondering what the other Barbie had that we didn't.

What's the moral of this story, you ask? It's simple. Men suck, Barbies suck, and there's no such thing as true love. Does life go on? Sure it does, but with plenty of tequila. This is my story.

CHAPTER 1

Sierra

I stirred when I heard my phone beep and I opened my eyes. The smell of his cologne first thing in the morning was nauseating. I rolled out from under his arm and picked up my phone, which I left sitting on his nightstand last night. Shit, I thought as I read a text message from Kirsty.

"Where the hell are you? I'm at your house, sitting on your unslept bed. Did you forget about the meeting you have this morning with the Dickson Brothers? They already aren't fond of you. This is your last chance."

"I didn't forget. Get out my black pinstripe pant suit and my black lace push-up bra. You know, the one with the extra lift? I'll be home soon."

"Look what I found!" Royce said as he held up the leather strap.

"Good times," I said as I gave a fake smile and put on my bra.

He got up from the bed and walked into the bathroom.

"Grab a cup of coffee on your way out. My maid bought some to-go cups," he said as he peed with the door open.

I rolled my eyes at his generosity and pulled on my skirt, grabbed my purse, and put on my sunglasses.

"I'm out of here, Royce. Thanks for last night."

"Have a good day, Sierra. We'll talk soon. Last night was fun," he yelled as I walked out the door.

James, my driver, was waiting for me at the curb.

"Good morning, Sierra," he said as I took the cup of coffee he held in his hand.

"Morning."

James had been driving me and my father around for the last five years. He was accustomed to me and my behaviors. The thing I loved about him was that he didn't judge me, unlike my mother, Delia. He knew my patterns and he knew my men. Shit, he knew my secrets. He was there for me during the toughest times in my life and he got me.

"Tough night, Sierra?" he asked.

I yawned before I took a sip of my coffee. "Isn't it always, James?"

He cocked a smile and pulled up to my house located in the Hollywood Hills. As he reached his hand out the window and punched in the three-digit code to the gate, I watched as Kirsty came running out of the house with her hands up in the air.

Kirsty and I were the same age and we met back in college when we were roommates. Delia was appalled that I actually stayed in a dorm freshman year because the Adams were better than that. I wanted the rounded freshman college experience of living on campus, even if it was just for a year. I hated every minute of it and my dad refused to let me move because he said it would be good for me to see the other side of life. After my freshman year, my dad moved me into an upscale apartment, and I moved Kirsty in with me. She became like a second daughter to him. Not only was she my assistant, but she was also my best friend. She grew up in a small town in Missouri and attended UCLA on a full-ride scholarship for business. She was incredibly smart, and she tried to her best to keep me grounded. She had a thing for James, and I was pretty sure he had a thing for her. Who wouldn't love her five-eight stature and size two waist? Not to mention her gorgeous long, brown, wavy hair and big brown eyes. She was one of the funniest and sweetest people I knew, and I loved her more than the world. When my father passed away two years ago, and I took over as CEO of Adams Advertising, I brought Kirsty on as my assistant. She already kept my life in order, so why not pay her for it? As for her and James, there was a twelve-year gap in age between them. She was thirty and he was forty-two. She didn't see anything wrong with it. I did because my parents were twelve years apart and it didn't turn out well.

My parents, Carl and Delia Adams, divorced when I was nine years old. They shared joint custody of me because my dad wouldn't have it any other way. I was his little angel and the only angel in his life. He got my mom pregnant at the age of eighteen and they thought they were doing the right thing by getting married. Obviously, it wasn't, because they always fought. During my weeks with him, he would make me come to the office to sit and observe. He always told me that Adams Advertising, one of the largest advertising agencies in the world, was going to be mine someday and he wanted to make sure I was ready for it. I learned the ropes, the tricks, the lingo, and then attended UCLA, where I graduated with a master's degree. As soon as I graduated, I became his right hand.

He was diagnosed with prostate cancer at the age of fifty-two and lost his battle four years later. I became the CEO of Adams Advertising when I was just twenty-eight years old and had been running it for almost two years. It was tough being a young corporate woman where nobody wanted to take you seriously. That was why I devoted my life to my career and my company. There were other reasons, but I'll get into that later.

"It's about time? Do you see what time it is?" Kirsty snapped.

"Yes, I do," I said as James helped me out of the limo. "Are my clothes ready?"

"Of course they're ready. All laid out nicely on the bed, waiting for you to change into them."

I walked into the house, set my coffee on the counter in the kitchen, and said hello to Rosa, my maid.

"Good morning, Sierra."

"Morning, Rosa. Toast a half of bagel for me please, light cream cheese. I'll grab it on my way out."

"No problem, *Senorita*."

I walked upstairs and opened my bedroom door. There, lying on the bed, was my pinstripe black suit and my push-up bra. Kirsty followed behind and sat on the bed while I changed.

"So, how many last night?" she asked.

I turned to her and smiled as I threw my shirt at her and put on my push-up bra. "Three."

"Damn. The only orgasms I've had lately were compliments of *moi*."

I laughed as I slipped on my jacket and buttoned the only button there was, exposing the lace on my bra and the enticing cleavage it created. I twisted up my long blonde hair with a clip and turned to Kirsty.

"Well, if it makes you feel any better, I pictured George Clooney fucking me in order to achieve them."

She giggled. "You have the most perfect tits. I wish I had tits like you. All I have are these size B cups," she said as she looked down and pushed them together through her top.

"Get a boob job?" I smiled as I put my feet into my black Jimmy Choo's with the four-inch heels.

"I just might."

"Bullshit. You're too scared," I said as I left the room and she followed behind.

"True. But then maybe James would notice me more."

I sighed. "Give it up, Kirsty. He's too old for you."

"Only by twelve years. When you're our age, that doesn't matter anymore."

I rolled my eyes, grabbed my bagel and briefcase from Rosa, and headed to the car. James opened the door for me, and I slid in while Kirsty got in on the other side.

"We're going to be late," she said.

"We'll be fine," I replied as I pulled out my phone. "Hmm. I have a text message from Don. He wants to meet up tonight. Apparently, there's a new art gallery opening, and he wants me to attend it with him."

"I don't like him," Kirsty said.

"You don't like any of the guys I know."

"True. But he creeps me out. He has those creepy eyes. You know; like a child molester."

I smacked her on the arm. "He does not. He's a good guy. Rich, successful, and a no-strings type of playboy."

"Child molester," she said as she shook her head.

Click the link below to download your copy of Then You Happened!

mybook.to/ThenYouHappened

BOOKS BY SANDI LYNN

If you haven't already done so, please check out my other books. Escape from reality and into the world of romance. I'll take you on a journey of love, pain, heartache and happily ever afters.

Millionaires:

The Forever Series (Forever Black, Forever You, Forever Us, Being Julia, Collin, A Forever Christmas, A Forever Family)

Love, Lust & A Millionaire (Wyatt Brothers, Book 1)

Love, Lust & Liam (Wyatt Brothers, Book 2)

Lie Next To Me (A Millionaire's Love, Book 1)

When I Lie with You (A Millionaire's Love, Book 2)

Then You Happened (Happened Series, Book 1)

Then We Happened (Happened Series, Book 2)

His Proposed Deal

A Love Called Simon

The Seduction of Alex Parker

Something About Lorelei

One Night In London

The Exception

Corporate A$$

A Beautiful Sight

The Negotiation

Defense

Playing The Millionaire

#Delete

Behind His Lies

Carter Grayson (Redemption Series, Book One)

Chase Calloway (Redemption Series, Book Two)

Jamieson Finn (Redemption Series, Book Three)

Damien Prescott (Redemption Series, Book Four)

The Interview: New York & Los Angeles Part 1

The Interview: New York & Los Angeles Part 2

One Night In Paris

Perfectly You

The Escort

The Ring

Elijah Wolfe

Second Chance Love:

Rewind

Remembering You

She Writes Love

Love In Between (Love Series, Book 1)

The Upside of Love (Love Series, Book 2)

Sports:

Lightning

ABOUT THE AUTHOR

Sandi Lynn is a *New York Times, USA Today* and *Wall Street Journal* bestselling author who spends all her days writing. She published her first novel, *Forever Black*, in February 2013 and hasn't stopped writing since. Her mission is to provide readers with romance novels that will whisk them away to another world and from the daily grind of life – one book at a time.

Be a part of my tribe and make sure to sign up for my newsletter so you don't miss a Sandi Lynn book again!

Facebook: www.facebook.com/Sandi.Lynn.Author
    Twitter: www.twitter.com/SandilynnWriter
    Website: www.sandilynnbooks.com
    Pinterest: www.pinterest.com/sandilynnWriter
    Instagram: www.instagram.com/sandilynnauthor
    Goodreads: http://bit.ly/2w6tN25
    Newsletter: http://bit.ly/sandilynnbooks
    Bookbub: https://www.bookbub.com/authors/sandi-lynn

Printed in Great Britain
by Amazon